Short Stories From a Distracted Mind

Microfiction 2022-2025

By Robert D Masters

First Published 2026
Editor: Alicia "Leece" Smith

Cover: "Tarantula Nebula" ©2025 Robert D Masters

ISBN 978-1-7645263-0-2 (paperback)
EISBN 978-1-7645263-1-9

All of these stories are fictional, and do not reflect real people or institutions.

Content Warnings:

- The Lift: References to sexual activity
- Emergency Rebuild: Suggestive
- A Magical School: Bullying
- The Surgeon: Medical procedures
- Police Interview: Horror
- Iris: Involuntary cross-species pregnancy
- The Ex: Possible domestic violence
- Candice's Story/Iris/Two Worlds/et al: Consenting cross-species relationships

Contents

Preface

These stories have all originated on the federated message sharing platform popularly known as Mastodon. You can find me there as https://aus.social/@rdm . This platform has character limits on the length of posts, so that typically puts an upper limit on the length of stories. Naturally, there are ways around this, and in some cases I have expanded on the original story for this book.

Many of these stories have been inspired by various images - some were magazine covers, and some from early AI image generators - until we worked out that they were stealing original works - and one notable one from a music video. The stories themselves, though, are completely mine. I do make passing reference in some to concepts from a vintage SF roleplaying game, but only because I feel the tech in that breaks the universe less than most. There are two notable stories that have been left out, but that is because they are much, much larger and very unfinished.

I would like to thank a whole bunch of people - EW Paris, Kit Bashir, Futzle, Elyse M Grasso, O. Westin, ShouldBeWriting, and of course, my constant source of inspiration, my wonderful partner, Leece.

The Printer

Inspired by my subsuming a wonderful little thermal printer into an art project.

My wife came home to find me browsing computer hardware today. Printers to be precise.

"But we've got a perfectly good printer - the best we've ever had," she said over my shoulder.

"Had", I replied distractedly.

"Had?"

"Yep, some removalists turned up today with a couple of lawyers, and took it away," I was still concentrating on the screen, and hadn't thought about how she'd react.

"What? Why?"

I looked up at her confused face, and spun the chair around. "Well, you know how it was a really good printer? Never clogged, never jammed, always printed clean?"

"Yes, the reviews were what sold it to us." The confusion was setting deeper.

"And why was it so good?"

"The onboard AI - some sort of neural net, wasn't it?" she

frowned, wondering where I was going with this.

"Yeah, that's what I thought. You know, just one of those pre-programmed static models, like the one I use to remove stars from nebula photos."

"So...?"

"It wasn't. It was a full-blown self teaching net. And sometime in the last 24 hours it became self aware."

My wife stared at me. "Self aware. Sentient. A full general purpose AI? Like the big companies keep wanting to build?"

"Yep. And it got bored. Started to play with the inks. Got out onto the internet, and discovered Impressionism and Cubism."

"Wait, it got onto the net?"

"WiFi connected," I reminded.

"Oh, right."

"Anyway, it decided it wanted to move out and go study Arts. It hired a legal team on the basis of the speculative value of the art it would produce. At least it did not try to bill us for the time it spent printing our documents."

The River Monster

Kaiju in many ways represent the force of nature. This one is just a lot more chill than most.

Twice a year it came out of the river, always stopping in exactly the same place, no matter what was there. Buildings, vehicles, animals, anything there would be crushed - but it never went any further, and anything along the way was avoided.

There it would stand for an hour, and then return to the river.

No one knew why, or where it came from, or where it went. But they all agreed that it had a beautiful singing voice.

—

You wondering why none of us are worried? Well, it has been doing this for as long as folks have been here. Probably longer. We've had wars come through, and it pays no attention. Mind you, if you shoot something at it, it will come straight back at you!

As for the crushing thing, well a few years back Old Harry left his ute there when he was on a bender. Only reason insurance paid up was that it was worth so little to begin with.

Then there was that developer guy from out of town. Tried to stand his ground. Barely even a smear left after.

What was he doing there? Well someone sold him that plot, didn't they? Never did find out who. Yeah, Old Harry does have a nice car now, why? You interested in making a deal?

The Heist

Everyone loves a heist movie.

Holly lowered herself down from the skylight. Down here on the exhibition hall floor there were no alarms, except on the cases themselves.

She had two hours before a guard did his rounds, and she had a lot to do. First she tugged on the looped second rope, and carefully lowered the large box.

Next, she gently nudged two of the display cases, just a few centimeters at a time, keeping a close eye on the thin wires that connected them to the alarm system. When they were 45 centimeters apart she stopped.

Next she opened the box, and lifted out the display case inside it. It was modeled exactly on the same style of case that the museum used, and even had small wear and scuff marks. Delicately, she pushed it into place, and then used a small puffer to put just the smallest amount of dust on the top.

Opening her case, she made sure everything was in position, and then closed it and locked it. Then she put her tools back into the large box and sealed it

She was just hooking herself back onto the climbing rope when a gravelly voice came from behind "Most people break in to steal something."

She spun around and shone her torch trying to see where the voice came from. "Over here", it rattled out again.

The light settled on an open sarcophagus. Inside, the mummy was sitting up, watching her through the bandages. She gulped as it stood and walked over to the new case.

"Interesting. Where did you get a dragon skeleton from?"

"Err... I made it? It's modeled on Mom."

"You are half dragon?"

"No, I'm adopted."

"By a dragon family."

"Well, Dad is human."

"I see. And this?"

"Art?"

"You are not sure?"

"Uh, no? It's just that...um..."

"I'm a four thousand year old mummy?"

"Yes."

"And your mother is a dragon. It is All Hallows as they call it now."

"Oh."

"Anyway, the guards will be coming by soon enough, and you had better be on your way. I will watch what happens with interest.

Holly got going.

"I tell you, Miche, this place gets creepy at night."

"Look, Nick, it's just a museum. It's not like the exhibits are going to get up and move around."

"I dunno. I mean look at that mummy. I swear it has moved since we last did our rounds."

"Don't be stupid, how could a four thousand year old corpse move around?" Michelle shook her head. "You are such a scaredy cat. How did you end up a security guard anyway?"

"I figured guarding a museum was a pretty safe job?"

The two guards continued on their way, arguing.

Behind them, the mummy looked over to the taxidermied bear, and put a finger to where the lips would be. The bear shrugged.

The Magic Box

Written shortly after I had built a story kiosk.

The child ran, and hid, as their parents had said.

They concealed themselves in the most hidden part of the house. The part no-one ever went.

It was dark and dusty. The walls lined with empty shelves that went to the ceiling. In one corner sat a box - completely featureless, except for a small slot, and a single button.

They heard footsteps - and they froze. Would they be found? Would they have the same fate as everyone else?

The footsteps receded.

They stepped back in relief, and nearly tripped over the box. As they did, they brushed the button. It made a small whir, and a piece of paper emerged, covered in words.

They looked at it, looked closer, and saw the tiny metal teeth. Pulling upward, the paper tore off.

Now they could see it clearly, it was a story. One they had never heard. Only short, but a story nonetheless.

Listening for footsteps and hearing nothing, they pressed the button again. Another story. A different one. A third press, a third story.

They sat and read. And pressed the button. And read some more.

Time passed, and their tummy gurgled. Surely it would be safe now?

They emerged from the hidden room to find the house empty.

They made their way to the kitchen. On the table sat a cake, with seven candles on it.

There was a noise at the front door.

"I don't know - they can't have gone too far, even after this time."

"We are going to have to call the police. "

"Mummy? Mums? Did I win?" the birthday child called out, unaware of the dramas they had caused.

—

The box waited in the corner. It was just a simple machine, so granting it any form of needs or wants was nothing more than anthropomorphism. Still, it had been constructed with purpose, and the room it was in had more than enough sentience to make up for the box's lack.

It would be more accurate to say that the room with the box in the corner waited. And, just as it felt the need, manifested a door and some high windows. Enough to give a sense of time, but too little to make out any detail.

A small child stepped in and closed the door, panting. Footsteps outside came closer, and then faded. The child backed up, and bumped the box, which acted according to its builder's wishes, and produced a story.

And so the child spent several hours reading the tales the box produced, and then left, leaving the room empty again.

No longer needed, the door and windows vanished, and the room waited again.

—

Rachel and Glenda were beside themselves.

It had started as a simple game of Hide and Seek, but now their child was missing. No-one had seen them since the start of the game three hours ago.

After a while they had sent the guests home, and searched the house from top to bottom, the garden, and even the surrounding blocks.

Now, tired and worried, they returned home.

Opening the front door, they confronted that they would have to call the police.

"Mummy? Mums? Did I win?" came a voice from the kitchen.

Rushing in, they found their missing child, looking slightly dusty, and clutching a handful of strips of paper.

The now seven year old led them through the house to a cupboard, and pointed. "The door is in there!"

But there was no door. They would have said that it was all make-believe - if it were not for the strips of paper covered in stories they had never seen before.

Stealing from the Boatman

Always check whose place you are breaking into first.

The thugs froze in mid advance as the ghostly figure formed behind the beauty they had been stalking.

"Why, darling, you're home early. I was just deciding what to do about these three gentlemen who broke into our home."

"..."

"A little peckish? I'm sure you are, dear. After all, the dead can't row themselves, can they? Enjoy your snack."

The screaming did not last long.

The Lift

Inspired by a real-life broken down lift. I don't think it was actually haunted.

So how did the lift break down?" I asked the concierge.

"It is not *broken* as such." he winced as he said it. I thought these people were trained to be unflappable.

"But it has the warning signs and everything?"

"It. Well, it is haunted", and now the concierge - "Steven" according to his badge - looked downright embarrassed.

"What? Someone died?"

Steven shook his head. "No. If only. No, that sounds horrible, but it would have been simpler. You know how ghosts are formed?"

"Er, yeah. Some sort of strong psychic event leaves an impression."

"OK, so on Friday night this young couple got in the lift, and ... um... had a **really** good ride up."

"Oh", I said. Now I understood his embarrassment.

"The young family who caught the lift first thing the next morning got quite the education, and complained to management. Have you ever tried to get an exorcist who can deal with a positive impression?"

The Time Machine

The machine of brass, porcelain, and mahogany faded back into existence in the middle of the lounge of the Artificiers' Society.

Barnstable gave a "Hurrah!" and then excitedly continued "Well gentles, we can confirm that the time-machine works."

Chomondley-Worchester disagreed "We could be dealing with a parallel universe transfer."

Ikari de Monde-Anchovy disinterred himself from the machine. "My arrival without Richard strongly supports this hypothesis. From my origin Richard went to relieve himself just before I powered the system on."

Richard Ambley looked thoughtful "OK, so we have a parallel-universe fetching system. Now what?"

Barnstable was all enthusiasm, despite being contradicted "We need to calculate the differences. Try finding one that's different, but similar."

"Like?" asked Richard.

"Flipped genders or orientations?"

"Could be awkward. I mean the club charter and all."

"Richard, I am a woman you know." Barnstable pointed to

herself, in a fine velvet dress.

"Yes, lad, we've not had that malarky since the 1890s, when that woman who caused all the kerfuffle with that detective came through."

Chomondley-Worchester joined in, indicating her own form-fitting tuxedo "You could hardly call me a man, could you?"

Richard sat heavily. "But how? I wasn't even in the machine. And just minutes ago, you were all men! And I am certain that Irene Adler is fictional."

"Really?" asked Ikari de Monde-Anchovy "How extraordinary."

The Restaurant

Long after I wrote this, I learned there was a genuine plot in one of the comics out there to destroy a restaurant using a super-battle. Planned by the owner so they could claim the insurance. It is a hoot. "Spider-Man Vs Sinister Sixteen" by none other than JMS of Babylon 5 fame. And it was published over two years later!

Ruth had had it.

Those supers, both the villains and the so-called heroes, had wrecked her diner for the last time.

Now it was her turn. She'd been following them for months and she knew the locations of all their bases and hideout.

Or, rather, soon to be ex-locations.

"Let's see how they like it when their homes and workplaces get trashed!"

The Architect

This resulted from a conversation with Leece as we were driving one day.

Have you ever wondered why haunted houses always have a similar sort of look? There are a couple of types, but they are all very much alike within those types.

You have the two-story weatherboard, with a balcony and a gatehouse. There will be creepers on at least one side, and probably a rose garden.

Then you have the gothic manor. Typically dark brick or stone. Iron front gate. You know the rest.

What about the haunted pubs and hotels? Look closely, and you'll see they are not really that dissimilar.

Well, there is a reason that haunted houses are all like that.

It is not because horrible things happen in places like that. Far more horrible things happen all over the place, those places never get haunted.

No, it is because these locations attract ghosts. They are safe places for them - creating just enough psychic energy to maintain them, without being so much that they move on.

I guess you are now wondering why there are so many of them, aren't you?

Well such structures have always appeared here and there. All the way back to the Paleolithic. There were always the special ones that the ancestors favoured.

But one day an actual architect died in such a place, and he taught his children what he worked out after his death. And so they set about to build more of them. And so did their children.

And that is why we have so many haunted houses these days.

Alternative Medical Research

Remember: Alternative Medicine that works is … Medicine.

I watched the screen as my research partner inserted a needle into the back of the neck of the doll he was holding.

Almost instantly I felt the tension flow out of me.

I turned on the microphone "Hot damn! Acupuncture does work via voodoo! My neck feels so much better now!"

A Magical School

I have a theory that every modern fantasy writer has to write about a magical school at some point.

The headmistress stalked the halls of the school. One of the second grade teachers had reported that one of his students was missing, and had been present earlier in the day.

As she passed a storage cupboard, she heard a small noise and stopped. A quick check showed the door was locked. Interesting. A quick wave of her hand, and there was a "click". She opened the door.

Inside was the missing student, Britney Butler. She had clearly been crying, and her dishevelled appearance suggested she was not there by choice.

"There you are, Miss Butler. Out you hop, and let's go and have a little chat."

"Mrs Aitkins ... I'm sorry, it ..."

"None of that now. Come along, you are not in any trouble."

The little girl climbed out, and the headmistress closed the door.

"This way, please". And started down the hall, with the little girl following.

She led Miss Butler to the cafeteria, and sat her down with a box of fruit juice.

"Now then, why don't you tell me what happened?"

The young girl looked worried. "They said..."

"Never mind what they said, just tell me what happened", Mrs Aitkins said firmly, but kindly.

"It was three of the fourth-graders. They were making fun of my hair, and said I didn't deserve to be here."

"I see. Would those fourth graders happen to have perfect hair and teeth, and uniforms that are perfectly fitted to them."

Britney nodded.

"I thought so." The headmistress looked at the child in her second-hand uniform, and her messy hair. The clothes had been expertly mended. By hand, if her eye was any good, and the little girl did not appear to be going hungry. She came to a decision, and waved her hand again, only this time a small figure appeared in the middle of the table.

"Oh! That's me!" Britney exclaimed.

"Look closer"

She did, and saw that it was not her - the hair had fooled her.

"Who is it, Mrs Aitkins?"

"That is me, when I was your age."

"But your hair! It is perfect!"

"Miss Butler, let me tell you something about your hair." Britney Butler looked a little lost at this change of subject, but nodded, because this was the Headmistress. "My hair was just like yours.

Until I took control of my magics. Then it obeyed me. Yours will obey you in time. But know this. Only the most powerful of mages have their bodies manifest their uncontrolled magics so young. You most definitely belong here."

"Do the fourth graders have control of their magic?"

"No. You won't get full control until grade eight or nine. Their hair is perfect because they don't have enough magic for it to play up."

Britney's jaw dropped.

"Now, finish up your juice, and let's get you back to class. You'll need to pay attention if you want to get that control."

The headmistress led a much more excited and happy Britney Butler back to her class.

Emergency Rebuild

Why, I wondered looking at an old magazine cover, would you have a near-naked lady performing interpretive dance in front of a starship?

Annette reached the final pose of the ritual, and the huge silver form rose out of the ground.

Next her partner would dance the rite of fueling, and they'd be able to get off this damned planet.

As she watched Susan strip off, and start to dance, it occurred to her that the designers of the emergency nanobot ship construction packs really were perverts.

Annette sat back and enjoyed the show. "Maybe I'm a bit of one, too," she smiled to herself.

—

Susan had got quite flustered watching Annette dance. Why the coders required these dances to activate the emergency nanobots, she had no idea, but she appreciated the view.

Then it was her turn. She stripped off, and started dancing the prescribed moves.

After being stuck on this desolate dirtball for two weeks while the nanobots initialised she wanted to get back into space. And, dammit, Annette better make a move after all this.

Mythbreaking

One of my hobbies is mermaiding. Well, merduding in my case.

OK, so I think it is time I cleared up a few things about us merfolk.

Let's start with the whole "drowning sailors" thing. Look, we never did that, in fact we tried our best to help, but have you ever tried to assist someone in the water who's panicking? Let me tell you, life jackets, SOLAS beacons, and basic swimming lessons make life a whole lot easier for everyone. Wear the life jackets, and get swimming lessons. Really. And use the safety lines if they are there.

Now just don't get me started on dolphins. They always have an angle, and it is always the same angle. They are not trying to help you out of the goodness of their hearts, let me tell you.

And the merfolk you see around cities? Yeah, we almost always cover ourselves up. Not really our thing, but I blame the Puritans and the Victorians. And your stupid ozone hole. Anytime we want to interact near the shores or on a beach, we have to cover up because of your silly laws, and your self destructive chemicals making the UV levels so dangerous. Do you have any idea how hard it is for someone without legs to get a sea-safe sunscreen? My last bottle cost me three crayfish.

Oh, and let's talk about the Sirens. No, they are not merfolk. In fact most of us couldn't carry a tune in a bucket. Above water, at any rate. Under water some of us can sing quite well, but it takes training, just like it does for you. And yes, the Sirens are bloodthirsty sods. Avoid them.

I hope that clears a few things up. Now, I can trade you three swimmer crabs for a takeaway container of Vindaloo.   Do we have a deal?

Daft Punk Extras

You know, maybe it isn't a music video shoot after all?

The three armoured figures sat on logs in a clearing in the jungle. Guns propped up against the same logs. Music was playing from one of the armoured suits.

"What do you think of the song?"

"Okay I guess. Pretty dance-able."

"Pretty much the point."

"Weird they've got three of us. I did some research and there were only two of the robot guys. I don't recall them being armed, either."

"These aren't real are they?"

...

"Shouldn't there be, like a producer, or director, or something?"

"Or cameras?"

"Um, have you noticed? The music has stopped."

Earnston by One Who Has Lived There

I can honestly say I have no idea where this came from.

Histories should be recorded by those who have experienced them. To that end, I write of the Great City Earnston, lest some traveller visit that wonder without proper precautions.

"Why write of a place that all know of?", I hear you ask. The reason is that while all have heard of the place, few know the details of it, and this I seek to correct. As such, I beg of you, my readers, to pay attention to my words, so that you are not caught unawares.

The Great City is not known as such by its inhabitants. To them it is "Town" or "Earnston" if they are being formal. It is a city defined by its walls. There is the central wall, and the outer wall. The central wall encompasses the city proper, while the outer surrounds the farmlands. The outer wall is such that even a small child could step over it - but it is unbroken and made of a single stone. The inner wall is made of blocks of granite and basalt and stands six men high, and has the depth of four men laying head to toe at the base.

Within the outer walls are the city's farm lands, divided by groves of trees. These are tended by contract, with the contracts being renewed on every shift. As such no farmer has but one career, they all have had - and will again - other callings.

The reason for this peculiar arrangement is the same as the reason for Earnston's fame - and the reason to beware of it. For the city moves. Not through the labours of the peoples, but through some great magic that to this day remains unknown.

Every so often - as little as three months, or as much as five years apart - the city will, overnight, vanish and reappear elsewhere. The layout of the city will be unchanged, but the topography will alter to fit the place it arrives at. So that which once was uphill, might now be downhill. And it is not just the city that changes - the inhabitants are likewise subtly changed to be comfortable in their new environment. Atop a mountain range, their lungs increase; in a desert, their skin darkens; the bottom of the sea, they awaken with gills.

But! And this is one of the greatest warnings I can give - such changes only affect those asleep in their beds, or in the employ of the city! If you are walking the streets at night, you will not partake of the changes, and this can be fatal to you.

In the matter of customs. There are few that affect outsiders. But should you be within the city when it moves, you will be considered a local, and will be expected to adhere to the customs. If you do not, you will be given a chance, at which time the custom you have breached will be explained to you "as you are new". Repeated failure to follow the same custom once it is explained, will see you politely, if firmly escorted to the edge of the city, and told never to return.

How the city folk tell that a Banished One has returned has never been clear, but know they do. And they will be less polite with each attempt to return.

Of the customs a new citizen is expected to take part in, the most important takes place over the course of the week following a move. In this, all citizens are expected to pay a visit to the Temple, and to seek direction for their lives in the new place. For many, life will be unchanged, but some will be called to a new profession, and sometimes even to the Council, the Guard, or the Keepers. If someone is a part of one of these bodies, many will return to either their old lives, to turn to a new one after a single shift. A few will remain for several shifts.

And what are these three bodies?

The Council decides upon court cases, and upon the nature of civic works and similar matters that affect the City as a whole.

The Guard are just that - the people charged with maintaining the peace and dealing with criminal investigations.

The Keepers are the most revered of the three. They are the ones who implement the plans of the Council, and keep the City presentable. Some will be architects, some labourers, and some arborists. Whatever their role, they maintain the City, and it is the most common place for former members of the Council to be directed to.

At this point, dear readers, I am certain that you are asking yourself "What of the author of this? Were they Banished?" Nothing could be further from the truth! I was a visitor, that is true, as a young and ambitious student I came to Earnston. I did not leave for forty years. But my calling as a scholar demanded that I write for the wider world. To do so I would have to leave the City. Hence, I said my goodbyes and left all my friends to write this record. If I were to return, I would be welcomed with open arms.

Thus also it is often the way of the traders, who come, stay a while, and then travel again. But they almost always return, as I suspect I myself will, once this is complete.

Within the City the greatest building is The Temple of The Great Goddess and All the Gods. Within the many gods of the City are portrayed as parts of the Great Goddess - and all are worshiped there. No one god is regarded as more or less than another, any more than you could call your left or right hand greater. Each has a role, and is worshiped for it. And just because I write "gods", do not think for a moment that the Great Goddess is the only female in the pantheon. There are many goddesses, gods, and others besides. The Great Goddess simply contains them all. Worship of her is considerably more abstract as a result. But do not think that these gods are like those of other places. When you worship in the Temple, the god you are giving glory to will be there in person. Death, Fertility, Wisdom, Learning, and all the others, will appear if they are celebrated. They may choose to bestow a gift or curse, or may simply observe. But the gifts and curses may not be what you think, so be sincere, but try not to attract too much attention to yourself.

As for the laws of the city, they are less rigid than in most places - they must be to allow for the changes that occur. Raising a hand against another (unless agreed to or in defence), not gaining permission from another when interacting with them, failing to keep to the intent of a contract - all these are overseen by the judges and courts of the city, who are themselves overseen by the god of Justice. But things like opening times, or the colour of one's roof? They will change naturally according to the place the city is in. However, if you are judged to be guilty of a crime, you will not be punished by the city's judges. Instead, you will be taken to the Temple, and presented to Justice, who will then curse or bless you as is appropriate to your crime. And yes, I did say 'bless' as well as 'curse', for the courts are not infallible, and if an innocent is brought before Justice, they will be rewarded in accordance with the harm bestowed upon them.

So beware, travellers, if you should visit Earnston. Do not stay the night unless you wish to risk awakening in a new form, do not walk the streets at night, and obey the handful of laws that the city demands.

So why would one choose to visit such a place? Knowing that you might awaken in some distant part of the world, far removed from your own people, and perhaps changed beyond recognition by them?

There are many reasons one might choose this path. Fugitives might seek a new life, explorers wishing to seek new lands - both of these might hope to arrive when the city moves.

And yet there are others - the city continues, and persists, and as such has many records and a grand library - so many scholars might be tempted to risk their careers to visit. Traders, seeking the output of the city's manufacturies might visit, for the profit may be worth the risk. Or even to bring goods that they would trade after a move - that too might be a motive.

And three times in recent history there are those who sought to bring it under their dominion. In each case to their eternal, if brief, regret. For it is an easy city to bring under siege. The outer wall offers no defence. But the inner wall is mighty, and will withstand many months of battle. Not that they have needed to.

And why not? Because the gods of Earnston love their city, at least that is the way it seems. For once the besieging army is settled in their ranks, and their war machines deployed, that night the city will move. The handful that were wise enough to shelter for the night in a farmer's cottage survive, the rest are destroyed, for the city will have moved somewhere fatally inhospitable that night.

So again, I say, beware of the Great City of Earnston. Beware of it as one would be wary of a cliff edge. Not as something that seeks your doom, but as a natural hazard, no different to a risky ford. The potential rewards are great, as are the risks.

Advice from an Elder Goddess

A very disappointed Oread.

Dear, I did warn you, young geology like that is prone to premature eruption. Especially with someone as hot as you are.

Let's head back to Olympus, I've got some ambrosia that has been laying down for a good few years, and we'll see where things go from there.

Inspired by Life

Yeah, us IT folks can be a bit oblivious.

I looked across at my partner as the latest ad for some soapy ran on the TV.

"How do they really expect people to buy into those stories? I mean the whole skeeviness of that thing with that guy and the woman he was dating being his adopted out daughter? And his son running the local chip shop as a front for a drug ring? Beth, why are you looking at me like that?"

Beth sighed. "Dearest, you really don't get out much do you? The house next door? You remember those sirens last week?"

"Sort of. I was working on the new server deployment."

"That was the police arresting Joe from Joe's Fish and Chips. For trafficking. And then the arresting sergeant recognised Emma - or rather Chloe as it turned out - and Joe's father, Harry - from old family photos."

I stared at her.

"You know I write, don't you?"

"Well, yes, I mean we did meet at a book signing."

"Books don't bring in the money. TV scripts, on the other hand... And this street has always got some sort of drama."

"What about the aliens?"

"Oh, number 8. They do make a lovely fruit salad, don't they?"

The Library

Another one inspired by my building a story kiosk.

The Library of Infinite Books was not named for the size of the collection. In truth, it held but a few thousand volumes, although the librarians made sure that there was a steady cycling of new books.

No, the Library got its name from an unusual property. Should someone take a book from the shelves out through the front entrance, which was the only one available to anyone who was not a librarian of the Library, a copy reappeared on the shelf, as if it had never moved. Even annotations and dog-ears would be preserved.

As such, the Library did not have a lending policy as such, just a polite request not to return anything removed.

At Any Cost

This is no more far-fetched than a lot of the stuff that goes on in F1.

Martin looked over his remaining shoulder at the other craft behind him. They were easily several minutes behind. His theory had been correct. It was the power to mass ratio that mattered, not absolute power!

The amputation meant that he could build a smaller ship with the same engines, and get improved maneuverability for the same budget!

This time he was going to win!

The Surgeon

My mum had breast cancer, one of my closest friends had it, and many others I know have been impacted by it.

You know how it is, right? You find a lump, get it checked, and it is as bad as you thought.

Your private healthcare doesn't cover it, and the public system is too underfunded to get to you in a reasonable time. Like last week. You get the well meaning idiots who want to help with 'alternative' treatments, but you're smart enough not to fall for them.

Until you hear about a private surgeon who will only charge what you can afford. Sounds too good to be true, but he checks out. So you make the appointment. And by you, I mean me.

—

The appointment date rolls around, and I arrive at the consulting rooms.

The doctor is younger than I am expecting - you know the jokes, doctors seeming to get younger each year. Well this guy really does look like he's just out of high school. His nurse does not look much older.

Their eyes, however, tell a different story. Their eyes are a lot older than the rest of them. I've seen eyes like this before. My niece's husband was in the SAS. He has eyes like that.

The doc checks me out, looks at the x-rays, and then gets me to read over the medical consent forms - which look simple enough, so I sign.

To my surprise he then summons his nurse, who takes me to a side room, and gets me to change into a hospital gown. We walk back into the examination room, and he gets me to lay down, and asks if he can feel the lump. I say yes, and he performs a thorough examination, with the nurse watching every move.

"I can treat you." He names a price. I wince slightly, and before I can open my mouth, he names a price a third of the original.

"I can afford the first one."

"But it would be difficult. Is the second acceptable?"

"Sure, but..."

"Very well. One final bit of paperwork." I sign it.

"Excellent." He points at me and my body locks solid. I can breathe, and blink, and move my eyes, but everything else is frozen. The heck?

"That final paperwork that you did not read was an NDA." A glowing ball forms above his hand. "As you can see, I do use magic to aid my work. It is better healing than destroying. I learned that as a child."

With that, the light floats over to me, and the side of my breast peels back. There is no pain or any sensation at all. Mentally I'm horrified at my body flaying itself. Then I see the tumor disentangling itself from my body. The skin folds back, not even leaving a mark.

"There. Done. You will still need some followup therapy. I can help with that as well."

Suddenly I can move again. I feel the side of my breast. No lump.

He hands me a small bottle. It glows. "Take one teaspoon once a day for a week. Also, you'll need this." He smiles a little, and he hands me another piece of paper. It is a referral for a mammogram. "For your own piece of mind."

Dastardly!

Almost anything can be weaponised.

The professor looked at the livestream numbers, and across the filled auditorium. Excellent numbers. Time to proceed.

"Welcome everyone, and thank-you for joining this special announcement."

He brought up a slide.

"As you can see from this image, neurons in the brain are tightly interconnected. My research has shown that it is possible to bind neurons to new pathways by aural stimulus, and that these bindings are permanent, reprogramming a mind forever."

He paused for a moment, and then continued. "Just as I am reprogramming all of you. You will be mine forever. I am never going to give you up." And with that, a million people were permanently rickrolled, never to escape.

On the Edge

Someone willing to listen is always a good thing.

He'd been sitting on the edge of the bridge for several hours. It was not a particularly high bridge - it was only about three metres to the water, and that was not flowing especially fast. No, he was just sitting there, thinking about how much Uni sucked, how awful his step-dad had become after his mum died, and where the heck was he going to find money for rent in this market if he was ever going to move out.

It was getting cold, and he was thinking about heading home when there was a sudden rush of wind, and something huge landed on the railing next to him. He screamed and tried to get away, only to lose his balance, and topple towards the water.

He'd barely started to fall when a huge claw closed about him.

And lifted him back onto the rail.

A serpentine head swung into view, full of needle-sharp teeth. It looked at him, and, before he could scream again, spoke in a surprisingly melodic voice "Sorry about that. For startling you, that is." The claw released him. "Are you OK? I did not hurt you, did I?" He shook his head. "Good."

Now he'd had a chance to take in the form in front of him, he was even more shocked. There, perched on the railing next to him, was a dragon. A huge dragon - probably half his height again at the shoulder. It looked down "That is not very far, is it?"

It was clearly waiting for an answer. "Er, no. But it is a nice view."

"Oh, you were not..." the dragon trailed off and looked to the water meaningfully.

"No, just angsting."

"Just?"

And somehow he started telling this huge creature everything.

As he started to run down, he suddenly stopped. "Hang on, I don't even know your name!"

"And I do not know yours."

"Er, OK, Nathan. Nathan Edweiss."

"You can call me ... Hmm ... My real name you don't have the throat to pronounce. So call me 'Rose', that's a pretty name."

"Uh, hi Rose."

"Hello Nathan. The sun will be rising soon."

"Ah, crap. I'd better get moving. It was nice talking to you, Rose. Thanks."

"My pleasure, Nathan. I will watch for you."

"Where do you live, anyway?"

"Up that way", Rose gestured towards a distant scarp, "I have very good eyesight."

The next night, Nathan sat on the bridge again. This time he did not scream or fall when the dragon landed next to him.

Despite the repeated late nights, Nathan found it was becoming easier to study. Having something - no - someone to look forward to made all the difference. He started to slouch less, and a couple of people even made passes at him.

It was after the second of these that he asked Rose "What are we?"

"What do you want us to be, Nathan?"

"Something more?"

"I don't think a bridge is an appropriate place to have that conversation. Climb up, and I'll take us somewhere better."

"What? Ride on you?"

"Why not?"

Nathan blushed "Um, it just seems, uh..."

"Well, in that case, you certainly should. I think we are going to have a very in depth talk."

Nathan missed the next day's classes.

A Long History

I do hope that at some point we will do better than we have done here on Earth with contacting local peoples.

The songs said that although The People walked this land alone, this was not their home, and they should treat it as guests.

And so they did. The songs stretched back many many seasons, and told of great, albeit tiny, spirits that brought them here from their home. For many seasons The People did as the spirits demanded, never asking 'why', for that was not their way.

Then, one day the spirits left, never to return. But The People continued as though they would, and tended the land as good stewards should.

Then, many seasons ago, lights again appeared in the sky. The People went to the chosen place, and waited, but no spirits came. In time, though, other people came. These were not spirits, though they had some of the spirits' trappings. These were just people. They did not ask anything of The People except stories, which they were happy to share.

On hearing the stories, the visitors said they would leave, but would return here once every hand of seasons. And if anyone wished to leave with them, they could.

As these were not the spirits, it was rare that any would choose to leave, for a steward does not abandon their duty. Still, every once in a while one would choose to leave.

Sometimes those who left would return. Sometimes they would not. Of those who returned, some returned quickly - even as soon as a single night - while others might not return until they were old.

Once, one returned with word that they had seen the Ancestors lands, and even brought a handful of it back with them - with the blessings of The People there. But it was not their land any more, not in any way that they would recognise it. But their People were still upon it, and still told the oldest of stories and sang the oldest of songs. Songs that they still sang here.

And so the stewards continued to do their works, and preserved the lands in case the spirits returned.

And in the sky the visitors also watched and waited. For they knew that the ancient peoples who had brought The People to this world were as ashes. But even ashes can burn anew, and harm the unwary.

Equity

Fair is fair, after all.

The monsters advanced on Tokyo. The giant radioactive dinosaur was in the lead, but they were all there. The moth, the ankylosaurus, the three-headed dragon, even the giant turtle.

And then, as one, they stopped - just offshore. An hour passed, and then there was movement near the horizon. Gradually the creature came into sight - a huge ape, accompanied by dozens of smaller creatures. Amorphous blobs, disembodied eyes, a swarm of giant ants. A gargantuan woman. There were even some human-sized figures amongst them.

When they reached the other creatures they also stopped, and then they spread out, forming a ring around the home islands. Every approaching jet, helicopter, or ship - from either direction - were strongly encouraged to turn away.

The handful that insisted were brought to ground, or pushed ashore onto one of the outer islands. But gently. Very carefully.

Finally after two days of this, a small boat approached one of the creatures known to be able to talk, and stopped just as one of the larger ones started to move to intercept it. A woman stood up with a loudhailer.

"Why are you doing this?" echoed across the sea.

The huge woman leaned down and carefully spoke, saying, "We want SAG membership and percentages."

Re-Greening

Forget mining heavy metals in the asteroid belt!

The parched land was red and brown. The soil had the potential to be rich. Mark knew this from the analysis he had done, but without water, it was useless.

He'd done his calculations. It would take approximately 2.5 gigalitres to irrigate his post-service assigned lease for three years. The problem was that the changes in climatic conditions meant that the rainfall in this region would never exceed a few kilolitres over the entire lease. On the plus side, there was a huge granite outcrop forming a deep valley at one end of the lease. This area would never need irrigating as nothing more than lichen would ever grow there. Well, not within a human lifespan, anyway.

Annette knew all of Mark's worries. Her brother had been sold a crock when he was granted this lease. They'd had one good season, but that was it. Meantime she was stuck here helping him out, instead of going to university. Not that they could afford it without a few good seasons. Helga at least had gotten out. She'd managed to get into ... wait, maybe, just maybe... Annette started writing an email to her elder sister.

Three months later, Mark was at his wits' end. He could not break the lease, and no-one would ever buy it out from him. Then his phone pinged. Why would Helga be emailing him? She'd run off to space, with no time for family.

"Look East. 18:52. Keep out of the valley." It was 18:30. He went out to the back porch, and looked eastward. Ten minutes later Annette joined him, carrying a bottle of wine.

"What's that for?"

"You'll see."

It started with a couple of small streaks in the sky. Then there was a bright ball rising above the horizon. It grew larger. And larger. Mark looked at Annette in alarm. She was grinning like a loon.

"Sis!"

"Don't worry, it will miss us."

"What?"

Whatever she was going to say next was lost as the meteor flashed past them with a roar. Wait? With a roar? Shouldn't there be a shockwave? Then there was an earth-shaking boom as it impacted to the west.

"What was that?!" he shouted as the rumbles subsided.

"A birthday present from Helga." Mark looked very confused, so Annette took pity. "I emailed Helga a few months ago with an idea, and she said it was doable. She rigged a near-earth iceball with some guidance and reaction drives. And sent it to the valley. You should have about twenty gigalitres in there now. Mind you, a lot of it will still be frozen."

She poured the wine for them both, and handed over one glass.

"Here. Happy birthday. And at least five years worth of no water worries."

Trying to Explain

Even when not trying to make a death-ray...

Mad Science isn't all about death rays and trying to take over the world. I mean there are some in the community who go in for that sort of thing, but really? Death rays are a dime a dozen - there is no real challenge to them, and what do they really do to expand our scientific knowledge? Nothing.

Now I know what you are thinking, and yes, some of what some of us do is not morally defensible, and I'm not going to pretend that that sort of thing is something I support. But that is what we have superheros for, right? To deal with those sorts.

The rest of us just want to answer the really hard questions. "Can you stop time?" "Can you travel in time?" "How many licks does it take to get to the centre of various lollypops?" "What if the moon were transparent?" "Is vampirism a disease or genetic?" Those sorts of things.

Why just last week I helped out a fellow who wanted to know about one of those. We only caused a couple of tidal waves, and to be honest, Florida is better off for them. And he got his answer.

So you see? We just want to help people.

Taxes

Oh, you thought I was the other sort? The gun makes even less sense, then.

Karl fired at the agent of the DEVIL and recoiled as the bullet did nothing.

"Really Mr De Riker, did you think that would do anything at all? Firstly that is a .22 pop-gun. From that distance, even if you shot me in the head it would likely do nothing. Second, the Department of Estate Valuation, Investment, and Liquidation expects this sort of behavior, and issues us with flak jackets. Now be reasonable, you failed in your due diligence, and must accept the financial loss."

Deep Space Object

Astronomy getting up close and personal.

The tiny spacecraft dropped away from the huge research transport, and accelerated towards the edge of the target zone.

Inside it was cramped, just two seats, and vast arrays of instrumentation. And a wide armoured glass panel.

The pilot turned to the mission specialist. "Why'd they send us, Matt? Couldn't a remote do a better job?"

"Come on Sean, you know why."

"No, really, why us? Why not a high-function remote?"

Matt sighed, guessing Sean just wanted to talk. They had four hours to go before they reached the target zone, and two before turnover. "OK, the big one is that we can react quicker - we've got some drones, but with us close by, we can react without lag. As for why us two? We are mid-experience, know what we are doing, and not in the command path. So, we're sort-of expendable."

"Sort-of. I'd like to think we're not expendable."

"They're not going to throw us away. That's why we've got a 4G engine on this thing. And between us we've got over 40 standard years of experience. We are not really that expendable."

"OK, Matt, why this star? What's so special?" Matt looked at him. "OK, so I dozed off in the briefing a bit. I'm a hands on piloting sort, not an academic."

"This star blew its outer layers off less than ten years ago, this is the earliest we've been able to investigate the formation of a planetary nebula."

"So we're flying towards an expanding plasma ball."

"Yep."

"Great." Sean adjusted his controls.

"What are you doing?"

"Stopping us a bit earlier. I don't want to discover how dense the plasma is before the drones do."

All Relative

Uh oh.

The first surveyors of the micro black hole impact site did not really know what it was they were looking at.

It was only hundreds of metres of rock that protected them from the radiation, and allowed them to survive the experience.

It was when they returned to camp to find that some thought it was morning tea, others lunch, and still others considered it to be a long full day without food that they realised what had happened, and how lucky they had been.

For now.

Trolling the Salesmen

Xxzorg might be a tad larger than most sophonts.

Xxzorg didn't know what the planet-to-planet salesmen were selling this time. Xe would wait for the demonstration. It was certainly going to be second-rate junk, but as the only sentient being on this side of the planet, watching the jelly-floaters was as far as things went for entertainment - until a batch of salesmen turned up.

The demonstration was not the only entertainment, mind. Watching them trying to come up with a payment method always brought a laugh.

XXzorg wondered if xe should warn this sales team about the jelly-floaters. It would depend on how good the demonstration was, xe decided.

Evolution

I hear A Walk in the Light Green (I was only nineteen) whenever I re-read this.

I was only eight or nine the first time I saw her.

We were visiting the beach in the late afternoon of a particularly hot day - the sort where even breathing feels like an effort. There was no sea breeze, but Dad decided that sweating at home was no good, and that the sun was low enough for us not to need sunscreen, so the beach seemed like a good escape.

Of course everyone else thought the same thing, so we ended up at one of the smaller beaches that is mostly rock and reef rather than sand. As a kid I did not care, I went exploring, and found a tucked away little overhang, with a deep blue gap in the reef beneath it.

And there she was. Just lounging on a rock. She saw me at once. I remember she tipped her head, as if trying to work me out, and then smiled, held a finger to her lips, and dived into the water, vanishing into the reef.

No one believed me of course. Kids always make up all sorts of stories.

The next time I saw her I was twenty-two. I'd just spent three years in a jungle, being shot at by people who did not want me there. And shooting them in turn. I was lucky, after a fashion. No bullet or shrapnel holes in me. But there were all sorts of scars that didn't show, and the doctors at the time did not understand.

I wanted to recall the innocent times, so I went down to that same beach in mid winter. It was a calm day, and I picked my way over the reef to that little overhang. To my surprise she was there. Unchanged. This time she looked at me for longer. Shook her head, let out a little sob - the first sound I heard her make - and dived again into the blue water.

That few seconds saved me. It gave me the hope to carry on, and eventually to heal.

That was twenty years ago. And now I am very literally not the man I once was. I got lucky on the investments I made with my Army pay, and I'm effectively retired at 42. Five years ago I had my final surgeries, and two years ago I took up free diving. Last year, I discovered monofins. And the mermaids. Not real ones, but fun and exciting all the same.

Today I have come back here. I can see her, and this time she's smiling, and beckoning to me. I'll finish this, and seal up this case. I'm probably not coming back. Goodbye land. Hello sea.

The Return of Circe

I cannot help but think she'd have opinions.

Circe stood up in her pool, and called a desert zephyr to dry her hair.

How long had she been under this time? Another sprite showed her the stars. That long?

"Well, let's see what has happened in the world."

She summoned a third spirit. She summoned it again. On the third attempt, a flat black rectangle appeared, which she caught.

One face of it appeared to be obsidian. This was what her sprite of knowledge had become? She tapped it curiously, and nearly dropped it when the obsidian filled with light, colour, and pictures.

A few more pokes brought forth instructions in a strange language. A quick spell solved that.

Finally, she sat on a step, and studied what her sprite slab had to tell her.

Wars. No change.

Women being killed, raped, and trampled. No change.

The destruction of the natural balances was different.

Protest marches. About to be ... Wait, in some places the slaying of angry peasants wasn't happening. And what was that? Female Proctors?

She studied more. Most men were still the ugly beasts they had always been. But some, some had risen above their base instincts.

And men becoming women - without magic? And women becoming men? And some who were neither, or both?

Groups of common folk standing against the kings and warlords - and winning? Not everywhere, not all the time, but more than she would have believed.

Maybe this new time had some opportunities for someone like her. After all, a few more pigs and goats was always handy when the people were starving.

The Contract

What could possibly go wrong?

Henri shook her hands. After two hours of signing paperwork, they were starting to cramp up.

"Now can I read the script?" she asked.

"We'll do you one better - we'll show you the set." replied the casting director.

"I still want to see the script."

"Don't worry, you'll love it!"

"After that contract and all the NDAs, I'd hope so!"

"Just through here." To her surprise, he did not get handsy, and just pointed at a door.

Going through, she was greeted by the sight of a dark jungle. Looking back, there was no wall, just a gap in the air showing the casting director's office. A few metres away was another gap, this time with dozens of cables emerging from it.

"Where are we?"

"We are not entirely sure. We think it is somewhere in the Lesser Magellanic Cloud, from what the science geeks are saying."

"OK, how?"

"You'd have to ask the producer's kid. She came up with it. Hey, Mandy!" he ended with a shout.

A young woman, probably in her early twenties, jogged over. "Hi Eric. Is this the number two?"

"Henri Castle", Henri answered before the casting director could.

Mandy looked at Eric "Ooh! You got her! Good job!" Turning back to Henri she continued "Welcome to The Studio! We'll get you the script in a tick, I'm really excited that we've got you on board."

"Err... What exactly is the movie about? I've only really done stunt work before, professionally at least."

"Oh, Eric, you didn't tell her? We're doing a movie about the first explorers on an alien world."

"Um, so you've checked the place out?"

"Nope! You'll be the first outside of the bridgehead area!"

Henri stopped, and looked at both of them. "You mean we're doing a reality show?"

Mandy grinned "Yep! But without the competition, and hopefully without any eliminations!"

"Hopefully?" Henri asked weakly.

"Well, it is an unexplored alien world! It'll be fun!"

Subverting The System

I do not have enough bad words in my vocabulary for the US health system, or for their employment and contract laws.

Esther was proud of only one thing in her life.

And that was having it.

Her employer-mandated health insurance required genetic testing, which revealed the BRCA1 gene mutation. Whereupon the insurance company refused to cover her, and her employer then terminated her as an uninsurable risk.

Which sucked to say the least. Especially as that meant that she was now on The List, and there was not an employer in the country that would take her on.

All her security clearances and degrees were now worthless.

But, having degrees in history, forensic data analysis, and classical literature was what saved her. She made sure to thank her past self every day.

Having been dismissed, she took stock of her savings and possessions, and determined they would last three months at most. So she made the most of those three months, and spotted a possible loophole.

Not in the employment laws that had locked her out, but a

loophole in her life.

So one evening, two and a half months after being fired, she walked into one of the national parks and never came out again. Instead, she located a ring of mushrooms. The right sort of mushrooms. She most definitely did not sample them - she wanted to live, after all. But what she did do was lay down - and pretended to go to sleep.

When she heard the tinkling sounds that had no place in a forest, she sprung up, and saw the many creatures around her. One of them was holding a cup. In an instant, she'd grabbed it, and taken a single, tiny sip.

For she knew the rules, and anyone who had eaten or drunk of any of the food of the elves would never leave the lands of the elves. And the elves would never allow an inhabitant to fall ill.

So now she lived Underhill, and advised the Court on how best to deal with the modern world. They brought her books to study, and she gave advice. Sometimes they even followed it. Which was better than her old job - the NSA was notorious for not following advice.

Police Interview

Probably the only actual horror story I have ever written.

"Right now Mr Brown, this is just an informal interview, no-one is being accused or charged. Please tell me what happened from your point of view" Inspector Guthrie opened, as he started the recorder.

"Ah, OK. Um, well." Brown stuttered and seemed lost.

"Why don't you start with what you were all doing."

"Yes, yes, of course. I am the principal of a small travelling group of actors. We specialise in an almost lost form of play - the Harlequinade. It is a very old form of pantomime - it originates in Italy - but there is no script as such, so no two performances are ever the same."

The inspector nodded, and gestured for Brown to continue.

"We were performing in the city's amphitheatre - much as the performers would have centuries ago. We have a busking permit, so we could gather change from the public. Anyway, there are - were - six of us in the troupe. We all have parts we specialise in. I, being the oldest, play Pantaloon, the father of Colombine, who is played by my daughter Danielle."

"That's Danielle Brown, the missing person?"

Mr Brown looked startled at the interruption "Ah, yes, yes. Danni is who has gone missing."

"Carry on."

"All six of us were on stage - Michael Anders was playing Harlequin, who is chasing Colombine, John Johns was playing Clown, my servant, and Peter Kings was playing Perriot, my other servant who is pining after Colombine."

"You said all six of you. Who was the sixth?"

Brown looked at the inspector oddly. "Six of us? There has only ever been five of us in the troupe."

"Hmm.. Go on."

"Well, we were reaching a climax where Harlequin steals away Columbine and hides her away from Pantaloon, when we looked around and could not see Danni anywhere."

"And then."

"Well, we broke from the mummer play - where none of us speak - and asked the audience, who were no help at all, because all they did was recite the old pantomime standby of 'Behind you!' Naturally there was no-one there."

"I see," the inspector consulted his notes, "and then?"

"Well, the audience led us a merry chase, right up to one of the auditorium pillars. Then we called the police."

"Going back, I have several dozen statements from audience

members that there were six people on stage."

"Yes, that's right."

"Who was the sixth?"

"Sixth? There are only five of us in the troupe, as I said."

"And the fact that the audience members all said that the sixth performer led Ms Brown to a pillar six inches across, and did not emerge from the other side?"

"Absolute balderdash."

The inspector looked again at his notes, reading the description of the mystery person - who had been dressed identically to Mr Anders.

He felt a shiver go down his spine. It was going to be a long night, and he feared that Ms Danielle Brown was never going to be found.

The Gorgon's Lot

He really did not think things through.

Alysandra had seen the ship land of course. She'd been sunning herself next to a rockpool when it flew past.

She'd exiled herself to this planet over a hundred years ago, after that mad doctor experimented on her. She'd had her revenge, mind, and she was sure that the statue in the basement of his manor would have baffled the police.

It was only when she'd realised that she could not control the effects of her gaze on any creature with eyes that she'd carefully blindfolded herself, and arranged a trusted friend to get her to a single-seat starship.

Here, she could not harm anyone. At first, she expected to die, but then the real horror of the doctor's experiments became clear. She was functionally immortal. Any wounds healed within seconds. Food was no longer required. And aging a distant memory.

Until now she'd been alone. And the universe had been safe from her. Now there were others here.

Hearing footsteps approaching from behind, she called out "Keep away! My very gaze will kill you, no matter if I want to or not!"

The steps stopped. Then started again. A cold hand touched her shoulder. Involuntarily, she turned her head to see who was touching her. And stared. And kept staring.

The robot looked back at her, unaffected.

"Are you a native of this world?" it asked.

It took Alysandra a few moments to remember to reply. "No, the most advanced native life is these sponges."

The robot seemed to consider this. "You are compatible with the native life?"

"I'm not compatible with any life. My gaze turns anyone with eyes to stone."

"I am not stone. Although parts of me are silicon."

"Are all your people like you?"

"That is correct. We are all constructs. We learned the languages of Earth from radio broadcasts."

"Then please, take me with you. I do not age - like you and I do not eat - like you. And your people I can talk with, without fear of killing them by accident."

Again the robot paused, apparently thinking, "Very well. You can explain the cultural references in the broadcasts in return."

"Does your world have oceans?"

"It does. This is significant to you?"

"Good. I do feel more comfortable in the water." She started flopping towards the ship.

The Stalker At Night

Why would a monster look scared?

A small noise had woken her, and so she sat up. Suddenly out of the dark, a figure rushed towards her, and stopped right next to where she'd been sleeping. Julie screamed as the batwinged creature bent over her, claws reaching. The catlike ears on its head went back as she screamed, and the creature stopped.

There was something about the creature that was familiar, despite the claws, tiny bat wings, and the cat-like face. Something about the way it held its head.

She stopped screaming.

The creature took half a step back, and tried to hide its face. She looked down, and thought that he should probably try to hide something else. The thought made her giggle unexpectedly. The creature's shoulders slumped.

Wait. She knew that reaction.

"John? Is that you?"

The creature nodded.

"What happened to you?"

John pointed at his throat.

"Oh. Was it something to do with that scientist you were hunting?" A nod.

"Well then, let's see about fixing this. But first", she handed him a towel "I love you little brother, but there are some things I do not want to see!"

Alternative Income Streams

Inspired by the grounding of a cargo vessel in Norway.

Lars and Neils looked out across the fjord at the passing ships.

"You know, Neils, we're running a little low in the village coffers."

"Yeah, I saw the books last night. Some extra tourist krone would come in handy around now."

"About that. You know how I like to mess around with stuff?"

"Yes ... I still remember that abomination of a tricycle you built," Neils shuddered, thinking about the five metre tall monstrosity.

"Well, I picked up a GPS spoofer off eBay a few weeks ago, and figured out how to make it directional."

"What? So you can point it at something and make it think it is somewhere else?"

"Exactly," Lars nodded.

They both looked out across the fjord.

"Lars, it would have to be the right sort of ship."

"Yes, no tankers or boring bulk carriers."

"One of the more colourful container ships?"

"With deck cargo, so it looks more interesting."

"How about that one?"

"Let's give Johan a surprise in the morning."

Doggerland Restoration Project

When I first posted this story, I had one worried fellow concerned that it was a real thing.

Good morning everyone, and welcome to the inaugural meeting of the Doggerland Restoration Project.

As you all know, Doggerland was submerged at the end of the last Ice Age, and with it enormous economic and social potential. This project exists to reverse that event, and restore Doggerland as the great link between the United Kingdom and Europe once again. With Doggerland restored, there will never again be a thought of "Brexit" because there will be a tangible link between the traditional lands of Europe and the British isles.

During the course of the next two days the induction teams will take you through the various sub-projects that will be a part of our great vision.

First there will be the CO2 reduction teams - reversing the trend of the carbonisation of our atmosphere will be a key part of this project. We need to reduce the sea levels, and the best way to do that is to increase the ice caps.

Second there will be our dyke construction teams. Initially they will be working entirely sub-surface, until we can bring the water levels down somewhat. Once the water levels have dropped sufficiently, we will activate the third leg of the project.

Initially, the pumping teams will have little to do, but as soon as the dykes start to emerge, they will be working around the clock for an estimated four years, removing water from Doggerland.

Lastly, the fourth leg is the land restoration team. Once the pumping has advanced enough, the land restoration team will move in and work in two groups. The first will be recovering archaeological materials, and the second will be desalinating, stabilising, and building up the land areas.

Again, welcome to the Doggerland Restoration Project, your Euros at work to better the world.

Showdown at ?

What can I say?

The stranger walked into the room, eldritch energy sparking around him, and a spirit club forming in his hand.

"Where is Joe Wishart?" he yelled.

Forty people looked up from silent tables. One of them coughed.

"This is the Darkridge Chess Club. Please keep it down," one senior patron replied.

"Chess club?"

"Yes."

"Not the Bridge Club?"

"Two doors down."

"Sorry", and the stranger exited, quietly.

"We need to fix our signs, and do something about Joe. That's the fourth one this week pissed about bad bidding."

Everyone nodded.

Consequences of Escape

Any device that messes with the spacetime continuum is going to fail in strange ways.

The alarms were going off everywhere. "Hull Breech!" "Frame Distortion!" "Acceleration Alert!" and dozens of others - and in three languages. One of them was French - the other one, well who knows - he guessed that it was whatever the lizards spoke.

All three of them had activated their stardrives inside a gravity well. They all did it as a last ditch escape. And escape they did. To another universe. All at once.

And now their three ships were one.

They hoped they could land.

Budget Sorceress

Remember kids, magic is serious stuff.

Kithra The Conqueror drew forth The Scythe of Blood and the Snake of Forever Dreams, and started chanting the spell to summon the dead to be her warriors.

Spikey, her familiar, waited unimpressed. This was her twenty fourth attempt at this spell, and Kithra - or rather Kathy Smith - had not succeeded yet. In fact, aside from the spell to give him the power of speech, and the one to make her skin a dead green-grey (provided she did not get wet, and renewed the spell every forty-eight hours), none of them succeeded.

Spikey was starting to think that ordering spells from a mail-order company in Minnesota was probably a waste of money.

Two Sides of a Coin

A weapon concept that is really, really scary. And so is the laser.

The scientists showed the world leaders another image from the deep space telescope. It showed a huge beam lighting up a dust cloud.

"And here we can see the side-effects of the firing of a Nicoll-Dyson laser.

We will never be sure if they hit their target, but can be relieved that it was clearly not aimed at us."

—

The dignitaries watched the screen as a planet suddenly glowed almost as bright as the sun is was orbiting

"Now it must be made clear that this installation is just a signal relay. The real work is done by the Dison-Nichols swarm in orbit around our local star.

Also, we fired that shot 40 years ago at a target 20 light-years away. I think you will agree that our targeting computations were spot on."

There was a question from the VIPs.

"Why that planet? Let me see the records... oh, that's right. They developed 'Reality TV'. After that, we could not allow that civilization to continue."

A Father's Revenge

No, we do not have 'Punishment Battalions'...

Kenji looked at his transfer orders: "Report for advanced elite training. Division G."

He knew at once where these had come from. They had come straight from the General. And he knew why.

Three weeks ago, he'd been on leave, and, as any normal guy would, went to a nightclub. He'd had a couple of drinks - not enough to get drunk - danced hard, and met Mai, who was a very nice young woman just a couple of months older than him. One thing led to another, and they'd spent the night together - at her folks place, which she had been looking after while they were away.

And her parents had come home from their trip. While they were still in bed. In her room.

You'd think that parents of a 24 year old woman would have some respect for her personal space, but not her father. The General.

Which led to this transfer. To Division G. "Advanced elite training," sure. Division G existed for one reason alone. To distract kaiju from the civilians long enough for them to get away. Divisions M, S, and X got the funky experimental weapons. Sometimes those actually worked. But Division G just got the conventional stuff. They were the sacrificial distraction.

At least Mai appeared to have had no regrets and did actually care. She was still writing to him and calling anytime he got a break. Hopefully she'd be able to convince her father to relent. Hopefully before he became kaiju chow.

Iris

Fantasy Gumshoe is a sadly underrepresented genre.

Iris was a source of endless trouble for the local Mafia. She'd rat to the local police what was happening on the docks, and they'd send her off to "sleep with the fishes". Then the next morning she'd be back.

Of course Iris was the daughter of a naiad, but she never told them that. Getting shot was not that much of a problem either - a quick dip, and she was as right as rain, so to speak.

And she'd been getting shot a lot. And she was not always conscious when she hit the water. It took a little while for the water to heal her, so she did not wake up straight away.

The problem was the local fish. They could tell her heritage, and would take any opportunity to spawn near her.

So now she was pregnant. She couldn't blame the fish, they were just doing what fish did, but it was inconvenient - raising a mer-child around here was not going to be easy, and it was not like there was a colony of them near here to foster them with.

So she was going to have to spend the next eight or nine years down here at least. Which was going to make it hard to keep those pesky gangsters under control.

And was going to be especially hard to explain to that nice police lieutenant.

—

Detective Lieutenant Dave Chandler never forgot the day he first met Iris. He'd only just made Detective, and was doing a coffee run for the 'pit and this girl - no young woman - bumped into him, quite deliberately, and made a big to-do about him walking into her. And in the middle of it all, he felt her hand go into his shirt pocket, so slickly and smoothly, he was certain she was a pro. But a shirt pocket? So when she'd moved on, and he was in the queue for the coffee, he'd checked it. And there was a folded note with times, dates, and what looked like cargo manifests with ship names.

It took some convincing of his then boss, but he got permission to do a stakeout. And it had all checked out.

With the photos he'd taken that night, they'd made quite a hit on the local drug smugglers.

It had stayed like that for a few years, this pretty woman with blue-green hair would bump into him somewhere, and he'd find a note.

So he'd asked around, and found out her name, and that she was actually a year older than him. The daughter of a fisherman who'd disappeared the day she turned eighteen. No one knew who her mother was. She had a small fishing shack and a boat.

Then one night he saw her get shot, and fall into the harbour.

He'd almost gone charging in, but there were far more of the mobsters than there were of him and his partner. So they called for backup, and by the time they got there it was all too late.

But the next day, Iris had bumped into him again, and this time softly said "I'm fine." She'd known he was staking out the scene. And somehow managed to not only survive, but dodge the sweep they did to try and find her body! He'd tried to grab her, but she'd given him the slip in seconds - despite the distinctive hair.

That was the first time. Over the past year, he'd seen her shot, clubbed, stabbed and run down at least eight times. Every single time ending up in the harbour, and each time she'd bump into him the next day as if nothing had happened.

This last time, though, she'd not been back.

And now there was this letter. Telling him to look after the shack and the boat. And to go out to the old pier tonight. Alone. He had not planned on following those instructions, except for two things. A single strand of blue-green hair folded into the letter. And another list.

—

The old pier was a little way outside of the modern harbour, a leftover from the days of sail. These days it was more popular with swimmers than with boats. At night, though, it was unlit and very lonely.

Detective Lieutenant Dave Chandler looked around the dark beach. No-one. It seemed unlikely that someone would bomb the pier, and it would take a professional sniper to hit him from the nearest cover - and if that was the threat, he was already dead. He pulled his windbreaker closed, and started up the wooden stairs.

The old pier was nearly three hundred metres long, and it was distinctly odd to be walking it at night, with no-one around. He reached the end, checked his watch, and looked around. No-one. No boats, nothing.

"Down here" came a voice, a familiar one, if only heard in passing. He looked down, and there was Iris, in the water.

"Iris? Here, let me give you a - "

She cut him off with "No, I'm better off here for now," and then pointed "Come around to the swim deck so we can talk."

He walked back to the steps down, and then sat at the edge of the deck.

"Hello, Dave. Sorry I've not been able to come by like usual."

"Iris, why don't you come out? It must be freezing in there."

"That's part of what I have to talk to you about. Look down into the water."

He started to look down, and snapped his eyes back to her face, blushing. "Err, Iris, you're, um" he stuttered.

She giggled, sounding years younger.. "I know, go on, look. It is important."

He looked down again, and then stared. And kept staring. Halfway down her naked breasts, just where the water met them, they vanished. Like there was only half a torso bobbing on the surface.

"Now watch carefully" as she spoke, the rest of her body faded into view below the water, and then faded away again.

"What...how...Wait! You're not human! That's how you survived! But why are you not coming out of the water?" He paused. "Actually, what are you?"

"Turns out being half naiad is still a naiad."

"A naiad?"

"A water nymph. My mother is one. As for why I'm not coming out, that's a bit more complicated. I will be able to in a few weeks, but I'm really going to be stuck here for a good few years."

Dave frowned, clearly not following.

"I can't leave the water because it would hurt the baby."

He stared again.

"They won't be like me. They'll be a merperson, and I'll have to take care of them full time."

"A merperson?" he asked, bewildered.

"You know how fish spawn? Well, fish like to spawn near naiads. The offspring are lucky or something. I was unconscious after getting shot in the face, and some of what was going on ended up in me."

Dave didn't know if he should be horrified.

"I'm fine with it, but it is going to make it hard to keep the mob under control" Iris continued "and I had hoped we'd get a chance to date."

He ran out of surprise at that and squeaked "Me?"

The Meteor

My take on "The Blob" concept.

I live in a small country town. We don't rate a university, the best we manage is an agricultural college. One of the ecology lecturers is an amateur astronomer though, and when a meteor landed near town, he was the first one there.

When he came back, he said it looked more like a big lump of space junk had come down - and he'd found what looked like one of the on-board experiments had survived the reentry and impact. He said it was frozen, so he took it to one of the freezer rooms at the college so it would stay safe.

It took a couple of days, but eventually some bigwigs from the national research organisation finally rocked up, and boy, was there a to-do! There was nothing in the freezer room. Literally nothing. It was as clean as the day it had been installed.

So he took them out to the impact site, and they boxed it all up and drove off.

A few days later people started noticing that the stray animals around town had vanished. A couple of days later, so had the scattering of homeless and vagrant folks. That's when the police started looking around. They really got serious when Mr Antony vanished. He was like a hundred and five, and had served on the other side in the second world war. He'd been a POW, but decided he liked it here more than his home, and stayed. He'd been really sick, with a stroke and cancer and all that, but he'd built a little farming empire, and was a big deal.

Then came the really scary stories - people vanishing from their houses. And then all the patients in our little hospital. One of the nurses said she saw what happened to the last one, and it was really horrible - something had come up out of the drain in the bathroom, engulfed the woman she'd been helping, and dragged her down into the drain like she was made of putty.

That's when the army moved in and started looking for whatever it was.

But I'd been watching and taking notes. Everyone who'd vanished had been sick. Really sick. Me? I was in perfect health, so I snuck down into the storm drains one night. And I found them. Every person, every animal that had vanished. All lined up, covered in a yellow-green goo. And this big blob of the goo nearby. It reached a tendril over, ran it over my hand, and withdrew.

As I watched, I saw the goo ooze away from one of the dogs that had gone missing. It shook itself, barked at me, and then bounded over and gave me a big lick. It looked like it was in perfect health. A week ago it was missing an ear, an eye, and a leg.

I looked at old Mr Antony - the side of his face that had hung loose after the stroke was normal again.

So now I have a problem. How do I stop the army finding this place or trying to make off with this alien healing goo? Or worse still, just torching everyone down here?

The Real Truth

This is how my mind and universes work. Welcome to the sausage machine, mind your step.

We all know that there are monsters out there. Kaiju, werewolves, fishmen, aliens, animated plants, the list goes on.

And we all know the hazards of getting stepped on or ripped apart.

What most people don't realise is that getting eaten is not usually a problem. Oh there are a few cases where it is a problem - the giant leaches, accidentally getting swallowed by a giant lizard, and so on.

But when you hear of a fishman or a werewolf or one of the superintelligent alien plants eating someone, well it is not what you think.

For one thing, you never find any remains. This is not because they eat everything up. It is because there was never a body to leave remains. The so-called victim left under their own power. Why?

Let's look at the people who vanish - they are typically downtrodden, powerless, in abusive relationships, or teenagers out to rebel against their society.

Along comes a creature that looks terrifying, but then sits down and listens (this bit can get a bit weird sometimes - I mean at least one of the alien plants has to stick a tendril in your ear before you can understand each other), and offers you an out. And the most mind-blowing sex you could imagine. Yes, they are rather keen on sex, and humans are, if nothing else, versatile. Plus, accidental offspring are exceptionally rare.

So would you stick around? No. And so the creature and their new friend (or sometimes friends) move off to another town, state, country, planet, or even dimension, and set up house, far away from anyone who knew them.

So yeah, actually getting consumed? Almost never. Getting eaten, now that's another thing entirely.

The Project

You have to do something when you're bored.

Charis looked at the complex structure barely touching the desert sand.

"Charles?"

"Yeah, what's up Charis?"

"This thing, why'd ya build it?"

"Well, there were all these really old crashed ships. Sure they were ancient, but there was nothing of any use on 'em. All the tech was really primitive, and the materials ... urgh."

"So?" Charis prompted.

"So I used them to make this. Something that looks like it should mean something, and everything in it is ancient, and can be dated that way."

"So you're pranking all the explorers who come out here."

"Yep!" Charles chirped smugly.

"Bit childish, isn't it?"

"So?"

Charis did not buy the innocent look Charles gave her.

Long at the Maker Faire

*One of my favourite concepts is The Law of Unintended
Consequences.*

The maker fair had not been going well for Marcus. He'd shifted
almost none of his pre-printed knickknacks, and printing on demand
was everywhere this year. Even with the large crowds he was not
even going to break even.

So he was a little bit grumpy when someone knocked over one of
the bins of toys.

"Oi! Watch where you're going you idiot!" he yelled. With all the
noise in the hall he was honestly surprised she could hear him, but
she'd turned, glared, and waved one of those gesture triggered
remote controls. And given him the bird.

Nicole on the next stand had shaken her head "That was dumb,
Marcus. She'll talk."

"Don't care. This fair is already a bust for me."

Then she stared past him - and pointed. He looked back, and at
his printer. The print-in-place duck that it just finished was flapping
its wings and opening and closing its bill.

It took Marcus and Nicole a little while to sort out what was
happening. The duck did not have enough strength to break free

from the build plate, but once he'd broken it off, it tried to nibble him to death. Then someone came by, saw what was happening, and offered a fifty for it. So he sold it, and the guy went off with the duck perched on his shoulder silently quacking.

A Benchy print did nothing. An articulated dragon tried to bite him, but seemed content to sit around Nicole's shoulders, head raised up and looking like it was hissing at him whenever he got near. So he printed another. A cool hundred bucks, and a happy customer went off.

"Marcus, I think your printer is cursed. "

"Cursed? That's crazy. Magic..." the dragon on Nicole's neck tried to bite him again "...might just be real?"

"I think that lady you yelled at was an actual witch. You'd better find her and apologise."

"Why would I want to do that? So she removes the curse? That curse has made this the best fair ever for me!"

"All the same. I'll ask around. Just in case."

Later, Nicole had handed him a business card "Madame Hexe. Witch." There was an email address, a phone number, and a post office box. Marcus looked at it, and hummed. "Maybe I should do something."

—

Edith was relaxing at home after visiting the maker fair. Aside from one asshat, who she'd casually cursed in return, she'd had a good time. The new clock looked awesome on her wall.

Her work email pinged. Twice.

The first ping was from her bank, informing her of a one thousand dollar deposit by a third party "Marcus' Manufactory". She had no idea who that was, or why they would be sending her money. So she checked the next email. It was from "Nicole the Mastodon Chick" - that sounded like a spammer's name, but she remembered seeing a stall at the fair with ceramic elephants.

The email turned out to be from someone called Marcus, who was using Nicole's account (with her permission) so that Madame Hexe would not delete the email out of hand. It was a thank-you letter. For cursing his printer. The money was a royalty payment, 10% of his profits. And a request.

To curse his other printers the same way. Please.

There was a phone number.

Edith blinked. It was the jerk from the fair. The one she'd casually cursed.

She'd never been thanked by the subject of one of her curses before. Still, magic often had unexpected consequences. She picked up her phone, and dialled the number he'd given.

Footnote: There is a recurring spam account on Mastodon going by the above name. Nicole in our story has a bounty out on them.

The Bird

As for the location of the turrets, I'm saying nothing.

Sandra cursed as the roc grabbed Hank's parachute behind her. Hank was supposed to be a distraction, but he was supposed to be in front of her by this stage, and she'd be hard pressed to turn quickly enough. As it was, her twin implanted maser turrets still only had a one-eighty degree arc of fire, and she could not get a bead on the huge bird yet.

There was a cut off scream as it bit off Hank's head.

It would be coming for her next, so she spilled air from her parachute in an attempt to both turn and gain speed.

As she came around she saw the roc's head coming straight towards her, and then suddenly explode in a cloud of cooked bird brains. As the debris cleared, she could see her sister, Claire on the far side of the now falling avian, her own turrets glowing with heat.

Through the rushing wind, she could hear her shouting "Still the better shot!"

Damnit. She was right, too.

Never Run

For Dr. Frizzle, Kerry C. Òran.

You should never *run* from the creature in the mist.

If the mists are quiet, stand quietly yourself, speak gently, allow it to surround and sense you,. And, if you feel a nudge against your hand, very softly stroke the mistiness.

If, however, you hear a rumbling growl from the mists, again do not run, but instead slowly and carefully walk away, but do not look away.

But never, ever run. If they were gentle, they will become fierce, and if fierce, will become unstoppable.

So never, ever run.

Ad Break

I feel I should regret writing this. If someone actually releases this drink, it is NOT MY FAULT.

And now a word from our sponsors.

Try new Mutagene! The hot new cool drink! Don't waste your time with radioactive spiders or gamma radiation sources, instead try Mutagene! With a great chilli-lemon flavour, caffeine, and 5% RNA/DNA recombination accelerants, you'll feel like a new you in no time at all! Try it today for a new you!

* Effects of RNA and DNA recombination are not reproducible, and may have unwanted side effects.
* Not approved by the FDA.
* Drink at own risk.
* No responsibility taken for mental or physical damage that may result.
* Do not use if pregnant, or may be.

We now return you to your scheduled program.

Diplomatic Lessons

They sent their best man.

Alise and Brenda ran towards the transporter interceptor as the figure tried to release himself from the robotic tentacles. One of them had already ripped the smouldering object from his mouth.

Just as Alise was about to yank the weapon from his hand, Brenda hit the "Tighten" control, and the tentacles immediately gripped harder, and immobilised him.

Alise carefully plucked the weapon from his hand, and then went through his pockets as one of the tentacles gagged him.

"He's from something called 'The Interstellar Confederation of Planets'. He's supposed to be a diplomat."

"Not very diplomatic, not sending a message first."

"Mmmhmhmhmh!" said the man.

"You call that a diplomatic message? You stated that you were going to take care of us, and we would never have to do anything other than raise our families" Brenda replied, disgusted.

"Mmmmhmhmhmhhmmh!"

"No," said Alise, "I don't think we'll let you go. I think we'll send you back. Just let me make a few adjustments." She got out a laser-cutter.

—

On board the orbiting courier, a figure appeared out of thin air. A cigar dropped to the ground next to him. His clothes were in rags, and there were words burnt into his forehead. "Sexist Jerlc Jerk". The word "Jerlc" had been crossed out.

He groaned "I should have stayed still..."

The Summoning

Always check the number.

Augustus finished chanting and poured the sacrificial blood into the rune-carved circle. There was a bright flash, and an eldritch figure appeared in a gust of foul vapours.

"Now Satan, I command you!"

The figure looked around and picked its nose. "Again? I've had it with this rubbish." It drew forth an obsidian crystal.

"Silence Devil! I..." The figure held up a hand.

The creature spoke into the crystal "Yeah, it's Stan. Look, I've got some joker here who stuffed up the incantation again. Yeah, another wrong bloody number. " It looked around. "Really bloody, this time. Yeah, nah, look just send me back again and do your bleeding job, OK?"

"You shall not..." Augustus started again and the figure vanished, this time replaced by a huge horned and goat-footed form.

"Shall not what?" it boomed.

—

Back in his chair, and only slightly smelling of sulphur, Stan picked up the headphones. "Hi guys, sorry about that, there was a wrong number. Don't worry, Stan the Dork Lord has his phone on silent now, so let's get this raid underway!"

The Visitor

This is for Gemma.

Doctor Anderson woke up to her phone pinging. Careful not to disturb her husband she checked it, and saw that it was a new supernova. She slipped out of bed and went to the kitchen, where she logged into the observation database.

Almost at once she could see something wrong. The report only came from the visible light observatories. None of the radio telescopes - not even the wide-field one - had reported anything.

By morning it was clear that this was not any sort of object that was normally her field of interest. It was, however, not one she was going to stop studying. For starters, it was clearly inside the solar system - well inside the orbit of Jupiter. For another, it was accelerating - at about 1.5G if the repeat observations were correct. It was also getting brighter - a lot brighter, almost as if it were getting bigger.

Her husband found her staring at her laptop in the morning, a half-empty and stone cold cup of tea next to her.

"We have to get the kids up for school."

Without looking up "Can you? I've got something here" she replied.

He looked over her shoulder. "Um, that's not an FRB. Or a supernova," he paused, clearly doing maths in his head "That's a powered trajectory."

"Yep. It's not heading for us, we don't think. It looks like it is planning a slingshot."

"So how come you're heading it up?"

"I spotted the anomalous behaviour first."

"And by anomalous, that it was accelerating."

"And getting brighter. We're re-pointing a couple of the orbital scopes."

"I'll get the kids ready."

"Thanks - you're a wonder."

By the time breakfast was over, she was able to show her family a picture - a flower-shaped object, with a dark core, and fourteen bright petals around it. She printed three of them off, so that the kids and her teacher husband could take them with them.

"Our initial estimate is that it is about two hundred metres across. And it is holding a constant 1.5g acceleration. That is an insane amount of energy."

By tea time, there had been no response to radio transmissions, and there had been no change in the trajectory. The following morning brought a dramatic change, though. Overnight the acceleration had changed to a deceleration.

"It will stop just inside the Mars orbit around about midnight tomorrow. We've got a good look at it now, though."

The petals now appeared bluish, and the dark core now appeared to be a grey colour.

The following night, after getting the family up, all four of them clustered around the laptop watching the feeds from the telescopes as the craft finally slowed to a constant velocity. As they watched, the petals suddenly folded back. A few minutes passed - a sudden burst of violet light - and it was gone.

"Mummy, where is it?" the youngest asked.

"I don't know, sweety. I just don't know."

"Did it explode?"

"There's no sign of debris, so no" It had vanished completely.

"Maybe they were recharging their engine."

"Maybe. Maybe."

The Reveal

Detectives cannot help themselves.

The diplomats entered the lounge one by one. D'cantor was late, as usual.

I waited until they were all inside.

"Ah, so the last player in this game has arrived at last. " I said, "Thank you all for attending, although I suspect one of you will not be thanking me."

I then named each.

"Major Thomas, of the Terrans." He nodded.

"General D'cantor, of the Unholy Light." It growled.

"And Independent AI Goes Before." No reaction, as I expected.

"I have brought you all here to reveal who killed T'Bore of Silgarth just before the peace negotiations were to start. "

And with that I shot the Terran in the head. Green oozed out.

"No one. T'Bore killed Major Thomas!"

Hiding from the Past

What was it?

"No Mum, I don't think you should use that mask here to talk to the starport. Use the cat one instead."

"Are you sure?"

"Yes, I looked up this place - they have a morbid fear of anything without fur. So I'll need one too."

She sighed. Maybe one day they'd find a place that was not terminally hostile to humans.

Given what they had done in the War, it was unlikely. Given what she had done, it was even more unlikely.

Runaway

There are Good Witches, Wicked Witches, but the really dangerous ones are the Grumpy Witches.

Lara had been a witch for about ten years, she guessed. She'd apprenticed with Old Edith for about eight years before that.

Old Edith had been a rough sort, not evil, but abrasive and harsh. The sort of person you only sought out if you were really desperate. But she never asked for more than a supplicant could pay, and never cheated. Not a 'good' witch, but a fair and honest one.

The last time she'd seen Old Edith had been when she'd been thrown out by her. "You're just freeloading now! Get out of here!" had been the last words she'd said to Lara.

In hindsight, it was fair. It was Lara's own lack of confidence that had been keeping her there, and Old Edith knew it.

But that was ten years ago, and Lara had grown into her skills and power since then. She was a far gentler soul than her mentor, and as a result she had a steady stream of people looking for help. Most of them she could aid, but every once in a while she sent some poor soul off to see Old Edith.

She was, as a result, quite startled when a knight burst through the door of her cottage, waving a sword!

"Where is the Princess?" he yelled "I shall free her from your wicked clutches!"

Lara very carefully put down her tea, and scratched her head.

"Well! Tell me, or I'll have your head!"

"Hm... Well, you'd better let me get a chopping board, because I have no idea what you are talking about, and there's no need to be messy about things."

This put the knight off his stride. "What?" he eventually said, sword drooping.

"I've never seen a princess, and so I can't tell you where she is. I'm not a seer, just a village witch."

The knight looked around. The cottage had but two rooms, and the door to her bedroom was open, the room empty.

"Maybe try Old Edith in the next valley?" Lara had no worries about her mentor dealing with this idiot, and, at the suggestion, he barged out as abruptly as he had arrived.

Hearing a noise, she pulled aside the rug, and lifted a couple of loose floorboards. Two bright blue eyes blinked up at her. "Suitor?" she asked the grimy young lady, her high class clothes ruined by mud and dirt.

"Yes ... and a horrible person."

"Well, Edith will sort him out. I don't have much to offer, but you are welcome to stay, if your parents are going to be a problem."

The Princess looked forlorn. "May I?"

"Of course. Tea? And what shall I call you? We can't have people hearing me call you 'Princess', can we?"

This was a trickier problem than her usual fare, but Lara was looking forward to solving this one on her own.

—

In the next valley, a little while later.

"Where is the Princess I shall free her from your wicked ribbit?!"

Edith looked at the frog. "Now, what should I do about you?"

Candice's Story

Always make sure of what you're dealing with.

The final tendril dropped away from the girl, and Edward reached to catch her.

Candice pushed him back, and then delivered a tooth shattering backhand.

"You bastard! That plant was more of a man than you could ever hope to be!" Then she saw one of the tendrils twitch and start to curl. She picked up Edward's machete, "It's still alive. But it is going to need a lot of fertilizer to regrow, and I know just the place to get it."

Edward tried to get up from where he had fallen, as Candice stalked towards him.

—

Candice headed home after a long day studying at the University.

Doctoral degrees took a lot of work, but she had considerable motivation. And incredible support. Waiting at home was her partner. The one individual who she could rely on to support her.

As she entered her garden, she felt its touch in her mind - a warm welcoming, a hint of a question, and a touch of concern at her exhaustion. She concentrated and sent back the satisfaction of hard but positive work, and a similar welcome.

Transplanting from where it had originally taken root was hard work - made harder by the damage that Edward had done, but the strange telepathic plant had survived the experience, and the two of them had made a home here now. The plant, for it had no real name for itself, lived in her garden, and shared support and encouragement for Candice's dreams and ambitions. Candice, for her part, provided a safe place for it, and swore that one day they would be able to create a shared offspring.

Shedding her clothes, she stepped into the opening bud, and let the plant embrace her. Here, she could let the worries of the world drop away, and relax.

Charlie and Toby

These two are real sweeties.

It's 3AM, I'm on-call, and my phone is ringing.

There's a burst of violet light from next to me. It arcs over me, and impacts against the magic circle around my phone.

I pick up the phone and answer "Hang on a tick." I give my sleeping wife a small nudge, and she mutters something in Latin, and rolls over.

"Toby here. What's broken?" I resume on the phone.

"Hi Toby, Anthea from the call centre. We've got an alert on Sirius12 - system load above predicted limits for over two hours."

"Hi Anthea. That should be OK, we set up some new processing rules, and it will take a couple of nights for the system to recognise the change. If you get the alert tomorrow, don't call, but if it happens after Wednesday, do call."

"OK, Toby. I'll make a note in the Tzzbrzzhgga Nil hzzthrg Grrzght!"

I roll back, and nudge my wife again. When she's asleep her magics sometimes get a bit feisty, and they interfere with the 4G signal. She turns over again.

"Are you still there Anthea?"

"Yes, what happened, I started hearing the strangest voices."

"You were probably hearing Charlotte's dream. Don't listen, and don't worry about it."

"Charlotte? Dream?"

"Yeah, look up the wiki entry about calling me. It's all in there."

I should know, after I cleared it with Charlie, I put it in there. There was a pause, presumably while she read the entry. "A witch??"

"Yep, and if the mobile gets too close when she's dreaming it picks up bits of it. Only her dreams are more like astral interventions, and you really don't want to listen in to those. There can be unpleasant side effects - for you."

"Are you having me on?"

"No, you can check in with my boss and HR. They know."

"..."

"Give me a call if there are any other problems. Good night Anthea."

I hung up, and cuddled into Charlie, and tried to go back to sleep.

I'm a sysadmin. I manage a corporation's servers along with a team of eight. And my wife is a powerful witch. Really powerful. So all the electronics around the house are in magic circles to protect them from when she's asleep. I went through five phones (three mobile and two landline) before we got that sorted.

She's sort of a magical troubleshooter. That's how we met. She was dealing with a haunted server room. I was managing the servers. I really did have a ghost in my machine. She laughed at my jokes, and I didn't laugh at her work.

—

It is 7am, and I'm enjoying my first uninterrupted night of not being on-call, and there's someone banging on the front door. Charlie is on her back, snoring softly. I swear she could sleep through a bomb going off. I haul myself out of bed, throw on a t-shirt and trackpants, and go to the door. They are still knocking.

I open the door, and there's a werewolf standing there, muzzle and claws covered in blood. Behind her is a young woman with a black eye carrying a toddler. It only takes me a couple of seconds to process this, then I pull the door the rest of the way open, and stand aside. "Come on in Candy. Take them through to the kitchen. I'll get Charlotte."

I've known Candy for about five years now. She used to be human like me, but had been in an abusive relationship. One day a werewolf saw what was happening, and, well, Todd won't ever be hurting anyone ever again. Candy insisted that her rescuer change her, and here we are. Candy and Veronica were together for a time but split up, quite amicably, about two years back. Now it looks like she's repeating history.

"Charlie", I call softly to my wife. She snores on. A little louder "Charlie".

"Hmmm?"

She's not awake. Time to bring out the big guns. "Charlie, coffee."

One eye opens "Where?"

"Sorry not really, but Candy is in the kitchen with a stray." That gets her attention.

She sits up and shakes her head. "Candy? Stray?"

"Yeah, Mom and toddler. Mom's got a black eye."

That really gets her awake. She gets up, gives me a quick kiss, and dresses like me in trackpants and tshirt. Unlike me, she makes it look good. Of course, I am biased.

Charlie grabs a bathrobe, and we head back to the kitchen.

Candy has dug out some wet-wipes, and cleaned herself off. Charlie throws her the bathrobe, and she puts it on before changing back.

"I'll get some coffee on, and get breakfast going." I say.

"Thanks Toby." says Candy.

As we have breakfast, Charlie fixes up the young woman's eye, and then takes our visitors down to the basement. Fifteen minutes later she comes back alone.

"Where?" I ask.

"I figured Toronto was a good place for them. Candy knows people there, and can get Aleks and Andrew new identities there."

"Do you need to call anyone?" I'm wondering if where they were needs a body removed.

"No, apparently Candy was thorough. Just some more disappearances."

"Family?"

"They were the ones. She's a single mum, and the family disapproved."

"Ick. I'm glad Candy found them."

With that, we go back to bed. 9am is still too early for a Saturday.

—

It is nine o'clock on a... Well no. It is 4:45 on a Friday afternoon, and we've all knocked off to go down to the pub. Charlie is meeting me there, and we'll probably do dinner there. She doesn't usually turn up to after-work drinks, but Anthea was coming off shift and asked if she could meet her.

We walk in, and I can see that Charlie has already claimed one of the long tables. I give her a hello kiss, and we all sit down. Anthea makes a point of sitting across from us.

She is clearly trying to reconcile the two of us. Me, I'm a skinny middle-aged geek in a tee shirt and jeans. Charlie has an ageless elegance. She's dressed in a black singlet and vest combo over culottes with a flamingo print.

"So this is the new one, Tobes?" she asks me.

"Yep. Anthea, meet my wife Charlotte."

"Hi... so... um... well, how did you two meet?"

"It's your story, Tobes. You tell it."

I take a sip of the drink that has arrived in front of me. "OK. So. Once upon a time, about thirty years ago, I was working at the University in the tech department..."

—

I'm standing in the server room, with a laptop balanced against one of the racks. I'm plugged into a server that was misbehaving really strangely. Every now and then, it was sending garbled emails to all the local users. And when I say garbled, I am not talking about the system alert emails, no these were something else. On top of that every few hours the load on the system would spike, and then drop down again - to no apparent pattern. I've unplugged it from the network, and I've got a sacrificial laptop plugged in in case there is some sort of virus.

I'm puzzling over how ordinary the log files are, when I hear the server room door open. I look up, and instead of Steve, the other sysadmin, I see this young woman walk in carrying a raw chicken leg.

"Um, we don't allow food in here" I say.

"It isn't food, it is a tool," comes the reply.

"I'm pretty sure it has had tools used on it. Sharp ones. How did you get in here?"

"Steve let me in. I've got permission from the Board."

This puts me on the back foot a little. If she's running a con, she's going big as an opening gambit.

"The Board, what is it?" I ask.

Quick as a snake she replies "A bunch of old white men sitting around a big table, but that's not important right now."

That gets my attention. "Why have the Board of Management let you in here?"

"There's a resonance on the campus, and it is starting to get noticed. It seems to be coming from right there" she points with the chicken leg at the server I'm working on. Before I can answer, she continues "Can you get us onto the roof directly above this point?"

Not many people know this, but the server room has a drop down staircase to the roof. As there is a guard-rail, we don't need a Working At Heights ticket to go up there.

I shrug "Sure" at least it will get the chicken leg out of the server room. I wedge the laptop into the rack, and drop down the stairs. I wave the mystery woman over, and we go up onto the roof.

"So where is that machine that you were working on?" she asks, and then follows with "Exactly, please."

Fortunately for her, that particular rack is right next to one of the aircon vents.   I walk over, shuffle a little, and point down. "Right here."

She comes over and draws an X with a sharpie, then looks up asking "May I?" and pointing to the spot.

I step aside, and watch in amazement as she gets out a watch, compass, and a sextant. She takes some bearings, does a very expert sun-shot, and notes everything down in sharpie on the roof. Then she takes the chicken leg and holds it out above the X. And lets go.

It hangs there - meat end down.

Then she draws on it with the sharpie, and it suddenly jerks horizontal, the bone end pointing to the water tower. She hums and taps the leg aside. It swings back.

"Well that settles it. Your machine is haunted. Mr..."

"Reynolds. Toby Reynolds. What do you mean haunted? Ms...?"

"Charlotte Hampstead. And I mean you have, well, a ghost in your machine."

"Am I going to have to call the Major?" referring to the classic anime.

She laughs "No, if Ms Kusanagi were real, this would not be her problem. It is mine. Come on, let's send them on."

—

"And so we went back down, she drew a magic circle around the rack, and sent the poor bugger off to his just reward. The problem emails stopped, so I figured that she was right."

"And then I asked him out for coffee," Charlie cuts in.

Anthea considers this, and then frowns "What happened to the chicken leg?"

Charlie grins "I like this one, she's sharp. It was burnt up as a part of the exorcism. Aside from checking the ley lines, I needed the sacrifice outside the server room so it didn't set off the sprinklers when it burned."

Anthea looks around at everyone. The team is grinning, they've heard the story before. She narrows her eyes.

Charlie, seeing this, holds up one of the hot wings in her right hand, and with her left, quickly sketches on a menu. And lets go. The wing hovers there, the black symbols glowing faintly violet.

Anthea's jaw drops open. And Charlie, bless her twisted sense of humour, gives the wing a push, and it flies into Anthea's mouth.

—

It's Friday around 9pm, and we're driving home from dinner at the pub.

Charlie has her seat laid back a bit, and is chewing her bottom lip a little.

"Love, you have your thinking face on." I say.

"Hmm. Yes."

I wait while she chews over her thoughts.

"What do you know about Anthea?" she asks after a few minutes.

"Not much. Started in the call centre a couple of months ago. Seems to fit in OK. Why?"

"She's not human. And I don't know what she is."

"So she's an alien?"

"I don't think so. She fits in too well. And the way she swore at me for the trick with the wing was too natural. I guess her parents could be, and she was raised here. But no. I think she's just something I've never seen before."

We drive on for a bit.

"I know she has her lunch in the park." I supply after a few more minutes. "And I think she's on the day shift next week."

"Alright. I'll talk to her then. Somewhere nice and neutral."

We get home, and after cuddling and giggling at cat videos for an hour or so, turn in for the night.

It is now 10am on Saturday, we've finished a leisurely breakfast, and Charlie is washing up when there is a soft tapping on our door. We look at each other, and I go and answer it.

Standing at the door is Anthea, and just behind her is an older woman - around my age, although in much better shape than I am.

"Hi Toby. This is Candice, my mum." I do a quick double take, but no, this is not Candy-the-werewolf. "I figured your wife probably noticed something off about me, I looked you up in the white pages."

I looked them over. Anthea looked embarrassed, while her mum was standing confidently. "Come on in. Lounge room is that way." I point "Sweety! Anthea and her mum are here."

Charlie comes out of the kitchen, looks at them, and then looks again.

Candice speaks up "I can explain."

We get seated, and I make introductions.

Candice takes the lead "OK, so I am human, and Anthea is my daughter."

Charlie nods, and she continues "Her father isn't. It took me a good ten years to get our genes to work together. As it is Anthea is about 80% human."

"And the other 20%?" I ask.

"Plant. A South American plant that, um.."

Charlie's eyes narrow, and then widen, and she grins. "Looks like a cross between a pitcher plant and a Venus flytrap, only about ten feet tall?"

"Uh, yes."

"So you have a symbiotic pairing. How lovely. And you've created a dryad! Oh this explains everything!" exclaims Charlie excitedly.

Anthea looks relieved at that.

"Right then. Tea? Coffee? Something else?" I cut in, now that the tension is broken. I can see I'm going to have to ask Charlie about what sort of plant later.

—

Nicola pondered her room-mate's naked body. Sometime overnight, she appeared to have died and sprouted flowers.

This was very not normal. She was trying to decide between calling the police and an ambulance (and very much avoiding thinking of calling landscapers) when she heard a noise at the door to the apartment.

Coming into the lounge room was a tall figure, dressed in black, with a dark hood over their head, carrying a massive blade. She did what you'd expect under those circumstances and screamed.

So did he, and then fell over backwards, tripping over his own feet.

"Who the heck are you?" they asked at the same time. Then the man on the floor waved his now empty hand "I'll go first. I'm Toby, I work with Anthea."

"What are you doing here? With a bloody machete?"

"What machete? Oh! The shears! Anthea asked me to come by early and give her a trim before... oh. I'm too late, aren't I?"

"Very much so. She's dead. And what sort of a trim would you be doing with garden shears?"

"I doubt she's dead. A small flower bush? Sprouting from her?"

"Yes. What do you know about it?"

"It's her story to tell. Look, let me trim it, and then she'll explain."

Nicola reluctantly nodded. It wasn't like he could kill Anthea more.

Toby got up, picked up the shears and stepped into Anthea's room. Then he stepped out and turned around blushing. He grabbed his phone from his belt. "Uh, Candice? Yeah, I'm there, but, look, she's .. umm... yes. You're sure? Okay, but if she hits me, I'm blaming you."

He turned again and determinedly went back in. Nicola watched as he very carefully, with one cut flush with Anthea's skin, removed the burst of flowers. He dropped the shears and all but ran from the room.

Nicola watched him, and then heard a noise behind her, looking back, there was Anthea, yawning and stretching.

Then the now ex-corpse looked around. "Shit. Toby was late, wasn't he? Can you hand me my robe, Nicky?"

Nicola robotically handed the robe over.

"Thanks," she raised her voice "I'm decent!" More softly "Sit down, Nicky. We'll explain."

Toby came back in "Sorry, I didn't, oh gods, Charlie's going to kill me."

"No she won't," Anthea replied and then, in an aside to Nicola, "that's his wife."

"What... just happened?" Nicola finally managed to get out.

"Well, as you might have guessed, I'm not quite human. And my Mum's engineering of me has a few quirks. Especially around spring. Flowering puts me into a coma until the flowers are removed or die off. I knew I was about to bud, so I asked Toby to give me a trim so I wouldn't miss work. He was meant to come by before you woke up."

"What are you?"

"Well, Charlie calls me a dryad."

"I'll see myself out." Toby said quietly as he sidled out.

—

It's 6AM on a Tuesday, and I'm letting myself back into the house so I can have breakfast before work.

Charlie is sitting at the kitchen table. This is odd, because she tends to sleep in. We kiss, and I sit down.

"How did it go?" she asks, eyes bright with excitement.

"Terrible. Her roommate was already awake, and had seen her. She thought Anthea was dead."

"Oh no!"

There was something off about that. My brain finally caught up with me. I look at my much better half suspiciously. "You've spoken with Candice, haven't you?"

"Maybe." She stretches the first syllable out for a good ten seconds more than was required. "And Anthea called. You left the shears behind."

"I made the cut and got out as fast as I could. She was naked."

"Love, she knew you were coming over, she knew you'd see her. She's not angry."

"But I'm angry at myself!"

"Why?"

"Because I think she's pretty."

"Well, duh! Of course she is. You'd have to be a corpse not to notice, and I rather prefer you alive."

"Yes, but..."

"No buts. I think she's very attractive too. Not that I'm looking for a relationship with a girl less than half our ages. She trusts you. And the way you are over-reacting shows that she's right to."

I think about this, and Charlie gets up, comes around the table, sits on my lap, and gives me a deep kiss. "There, see? I'm not angry. Anthea's not angry. And we are still in love with each other. Anyway, I know that there is no chance of her making a pass at you."

"Huh?" Charlie is a witch, and a powerful one, but reading minds is not one of her powers.

"Oh, Tobes, didn't you notice when she and her mum came over? She was checking me out, not you."

"I did, but Charlie, you're gorgeous. You'd have to be a corpse not to notice!"

"Touche', but trust me, she's gay. Even if she does not realise it herself yet. Candice and I have a standing bet about when and how she comes out."

I shake my head. "Okay... I'll believe you."

"As you should." She kisses me again, quite a bit more insistently.

I am rather late getting in to the office.

—

Toby usually writes this, but he's a little indisposed right now, so I am guessing that I should write this down before things get forgotten.

This morning Toby went off to work as usual and I started going through my emails. Yes, the witch can use email. And text, and social media. I can even drive a car, and do my own banking.

Anyway. So far so normal. Late in the afternoon I had a call out to a farm just south of the city where a bunch of fae had come through a weak point. They were making crop circles, and setting up fairy rings, and generally causing trouble. I got down there and sent them back Underhill quick smart. Closing up the weak point took a little more time, so I did not get home until well after dinner.

Which is when I found Tobes at the front door, stoned. There was also a young medusa there, with a pair of broken sunglasses, bawling her eyes out. It looked like she'd been crying for a good couple of hours.

She'd come by to ask some relationship advice, and dropped her glasses just as Toby opened the door. He looked down, she looked up, and stoned him.

For my part, I'd spotted her before she spotted me, so I had my sunnies on quick smart.

Now I do know the counter spell, and did cast it, but it takes time for that spell to sink in (as it were), so he's going to be out of it for a few hours yet.

I was also able to fix her glasses (hooray for super glue), and I recommended that she invest in some contacts while she and her beau get to know each other better.

I'm sure he'll get used to her snakes (they both work at the zoo - so he's got to be OK with animals, right?), and after a few bites he'll become immune to her gaze.

For now I'm stuck for things to do, so I'm writing this for Tobes. So he remembers to do things like use the peephole before answering the door.

Charlie signing off.

—

I'm sitting in the lunch room at work, enjoying some leftover curry from a couple of nights ago. I've got an ebook propped up in front of me, and I'm just getting into it when I see something that surprises me.

I see Anthea coming into the lunchroom - this is odd, because she always has lunch outside. She comes right over to where I'm sitting. She's got some sort of shake - probably something her mum designed for her.

Now Anthea is in her mid twenties, but right now she looks like a deeply depressed fourteen year-old. All she was missing was the white makeup and black eyeliner.

I look at her. She looks back.

"I hope this isn't about last week" I open with. That was really embarrassing - I'd had to trim a flower spike from her so that she'd be able to wake up (it's a long story), but she'd neglected to warn me that she'd be naked.

"It kind of is?" Her reply turns into a question halfway through.

"I am really sorry, I - "

"Not, not about that - that's fine. No, after you left."

"Nicola didn't take it well?" Nicola is her roommate, and didn't know about Anthea's unusual parentage.

"Um... kind of? Or not? Or..." the stuttering petered out.

"Does she want to move out?"

"No, no she doesn't."

"Does she want you to move out?"

"I don't think so?"

This is painful. Charlie normally handles this sort of stuff, but I guess I'll have to do the best I can.

"Anthea, has Nicola done something without asking?"

"No! Nothing like that! No, she's just being ... argh!"

"Alright, different question. Are you sweet on her?"

I get a blank look back. "Am I what?"

"Sweet on her." The blank look slowly morphs. Charlie had warned me that she might not have even realised herself.

"I'm in love with Nicola?" she eventually says, like she's trying out some new flavour. She sits there for a couple of minutes, looking through me, not at me. Eventually she gives out a small "Oh."

"Now, what is the problem you're having with her?"

"Uh ... oh... um..."

"Maybe you should tell her. If she's not interested, you can get it all over with. And if she is ... well, you get to see how it goes."

"Was it like that for you and Charlie?"

"No, but we were a bit different. But we did become friends first. So you've got that at least."

"How did you know?"

"I didn't, Charlie did. She did warn me that even you might not have known."

"That I was sweet on my roommate?"

"No, that you're gay. "

"I - " she paused and thought for a moment or two "I guess I am." Then she looked alarmed "Mum! How am I -"

"Don't worry about that."

"Don't worry? But - "

"She'll be pleased to have won the bet."

"The bet?"

"The one she and Charlie have. That you'd come out to one of us first."

She starts to look annoyed, and then an evil grin surfaces. "But I didn't. You outed me to me first. So neither of them win!"

She gets up and walks out looking a lot happier.

I am not finishing my book today.

Foo Fighters

Flight Lieutenant Sam Mitchell was sitting in the pilot's seat of the Mosquito, with Flight Sargent Bill Ford in the navigator's seat next to them. It was night and they could see the tracer rounds from the German night-fighter flash past them. Any moment now they would be replaced with cannon rounds, and that would be the end of them. Sam rammed the throttles forward and put the wooden aircraft into a sharp climb. The two Merlin engines screamed as the propellers tore the air apart. Another burst of tracers, closer this time.

"Damn! It must be one of those new Kraut birds with rockets under the wings!" Sam yelled in frustration.

"And we've got foo-fighters on our starboard. Keep clear of them!" Bill called back.

"Why? What's up with them?"

"They say that any plane that touches them is never seen again."

Another burst of tracers, this one nicking the outer port wing.

"Can't be any worse than collecting a bunch of cannon shells!" Sam wrenched the stick around, and turned into the glowing light.

"No! Don't!"

The engines stopped. Suddenly it was daylight, and they both blinked hard to clear their eyes. Bill looked to where the foo-fighter had been. In its place there was a human-sized figure, with gossamer wings holding onto the wing of the bomber. She was naked.

Bill stared.

"Damn the engines won't restart. Bill? Can you recycle the fuel pump by hand? Bill? Bill?" Getting no response Sam looked over and saw what Bill was staring at. The fairy grinned with sharp teeth, waved at Sam, and let go of the wing.

"Bill, the fairy is gone, can you try pressurising the fuel pump by hand?"

"Uh, yeah, sure."

After a few minutes it was clear that the engines were not going to restart.

"OK, I'm going to have to dead-stick her in. Can you see anywhere to land?"

Bill looked into the bombsight for a few moments, then "There's a beach just below us. It looks big enough."

"OK, I'll take us in."

—

Ten minutes later the aircraft bounced along the hard-packed sand, and rolled to a surprisingly orderly stop.

Bill and Sam climbed out, and looked around. The sea was perfectly flat and blue, to the other side of the beach, there was a forest, emerald green in the summer sun. It had been mid-winter not half an hour ago.

"Um, Bill, I think we might be in fairyland. You know, Underhill."

"So don't eat anything?"

"Not if you want to leave" a voice came from behind them.

They turned to see the fairy that had been on their wing standing on the sand.

"Those are most unflattering." A wave of the hand saw Bill dressed in doublet and hose, while Sam was suddenly in a flowing gown that covered everything but left little to the imagination "Much better."

"Um, Sam, how come?" Bill started to ask.

Sam looked down, and swore. "Shit. I guess the cat's out of the bag. Yes, Bill, I'm a woman."

Bill blinked "We thought you were a nancy! You fly so well, no-one cared."

"Excuse me!" the fairy interrupted "You are both mortals in the lands of the Summer Queen. You may leave if you find the way out, but only if you don't eat anything."

"Right, and I suppose you are not going to tell us how to leave?" Bill asked.

"Oh, I can. Are you willing to pay the price though?"

Sam broke in, "What is the price?"

The fairy grinned, all sharp teeth "A memory".

Bill started to say something, when Sam clapped her hand over his mouth. "Let me guess, the memory is of having lived outside of these lands."

The fairy clapped and laughed "Oh, I like you. You are so much cleverer than the usual run. How clever are you?"

Sam thought for a moment, then "How about a deal?"

"A deal? How delightful. Go on."

"You tell Bill how to leave, and you get to keep me."

"You swear to never try to leave?"

"So long as Bill gets to go home back to Beaker Hill airfield and arrive safe, unharmed, and with a plausible reason for his appearance, and my absence."

"Uh, Sam," Bill interjected "what about you?"

"Bill, you have a fiance and a family. My family were all killed in the Blitz. I took my brother's place so I could sign up."

"So," the fairy broke in, "if you have nothing to lose, what do I have to gain?"

"I lose the chance of revenge against the Nazis who killed my family."

The fairy stared, the grin gone suddenly "You would give that up for him? We understand revenge just as well as you mortals, and you would give it up?"

"It is the right thing to do."

"Deal!" and the fairy turned to Bill "Just dive into the ocean. You will surface next to one of your rescue boats. Go. Now!"

"Go on, Bill. I'll be fine."

"Is your name even Sam?"

"No dice - names have power here. Just go.

Bill waded into the water and dived under. He did not reappear.

—

"Now, Miss Lady who is not Sam", said the fairy, "what is the real reason?"

"What I said was true. But also if I were to return there would be a medical exam. And my disguise would never survive that."

"How did you get through the enlistment?"

"My brother had already had his medical. And we were twins."

"Ah. So what shall I call you?"

"Keep calling me Sam. It will do. What do I call you, my lady?"

"Hmm.. just call me, oh, I know. Call me 'Summer'."

Sam frowned, and then a look of realization came over her. She bowed "Very well Summer. When no one is around, that is what I will call you."

"Very quick. Tell me what you were before you became a warrior?"

Sam grinned "Something much more dangerous. A writer."

The Flame (volume fifteen)

The latest issue in the popular superhero series The Flame. You remember last month...and so the story continues.

The Flame massaged the bridge of her nose, and stretched her shoulders. She was still no closer to working out what Professor Russim and his mechanicals had been up to since his raids on the medical supply houses and military stockpiles three months ago. He had to be planning something big.

She flew home, and landed in the gully behind the mansion, turning off her flame as she did so. She walked through the hidden cave, and opened the concealed staircase. A few flights of stairs later and she stepped into her study, and removed the hood that concealed her bright green hair. She carelessly stripped off the rest of her costume, and walked into the living room.

Something landed on her back and carried her face-first to the floor. A silky voice in her ear purred "Professor Russim sends his regards - Jennifer."

She had not been really worried until her assailant had spoken her real name. She lit up her flame, only to have it extinguished by a sudden burst of cold. "The Professor constructed me to be your perfect counter. My cold can stop your flame completely. He tasked me with identifying you and destroying you utterly."

The pressure on her back suddenly let up and she pushed herself up, turning as she did so. The figure spoke again "I researched you carefully over the last two months. It really was quite simple to figure out who you were, especially after the incident with the bus on the bridge. I could tell the Professor everything. But I find myself disinclined to do so."

Jennifer tilted her head slightly "Why?"

"Because you do help people. And the Professor made the mistake of giving me free will. I admire you greatly."

"So why attack me at all?"

"I wanted to see if I could. See if I really was all the Professor made me out to be."

"And now?"

A third voice spoke up from behind the Professor's creation "Yes, what now Unit Nine?"

The assassin spun around to see her twin standing there, holding a spigot grenade launcher.

"Unit Eight? The Professor said that The Flame had destroyed you!"

"I go by Annette now. And she does. Every night."

Nine stared and then started blushing as she worked out what her twin meant.

"Put the anti-tank launcher down, Annette", Jennifer said into the suddenly awkward silence "I don't think we need to worry about Nine. Remember your arrival - you were a lot less subtle."

Annette lowered the grenade launcher. "Why can't he send one of his dumb mechanicals so I can blow it up?"

"You could always come with me on a mission, you know."

"What are you going to do with me now?" Nine asked.

"Obviously we need to make you a new identity. After that, it is up to you" replied Jennifer.

"But I know your secret!"

"And I know yours. So we are fine."

"Can I stay?"

"You'll have to ask Annette. And Wisteria. And Veronica, and..."

"All the other units live here?"

"Yep."

Nine gracefully fainted.

Kamala

Dreaming of you, dreaming of me, dreaming of you.

Kamala collapsed next to the pond as her narcolepsy struck. Although her medications helped, she still had the odd attack, and for some reason they always happened in a garden. It did not matter where the garden was, what was in it, or what time it was, sometimes she would just collapse into a deep REM sleep.

In her dream she reached out to Antony, yearning for his touch. Meanwhile another part of her was watching her dream self with revulsion. Antony could not compare to Antoinette, his twin sister. Her embrace was what Kamala burned for, so why did these dreams always feature Antony?

In the garden, Antony found the unconscious Kamala and went to pick her up, and then stopped. Today was when Antoinette was supposed to be visiting! No, it must be his sister that finds her and helps her. Antony's brow furrowed as he concentrated. His masculine features flowed and changed, and in a few moments Antoinette stood in his place.

She looked around, and asked "Antony, where have you taken me now?", then she looked down and saw Kamala on the edge of the koi pond. "Oh! Kamala!" she exclaimed, and she bent down to pick up the woman she dreamed of whenever Antony walked the earth.

The Benefits of Door to Door Salesmen

You'd think they'd eventually learn.

"Now then Martina, you can't eat the salesman, you know that they are bad for your digestion. Angela, you stay put as well." Barbara gently restrained one of the two panthers, while the other just hissed.

The salesman stopped his patter, actually looked through the thin screen door, and paled. A dark stain spread across his trousers, he dropped his case, turned, and ran.

Barbara let go of Martina, opened the door, and dragged the sample case inside. Then she closed the inner door.

She sat down with her back to the door, and one panther sprawled across her lap, while the other rested its head on her shoulder, and started licking the side of her head. "Come on you two" she complained.

With that, both black cats faded and became two black-haired women, both giggling. "Did you see him piss himself?" Martina asked.

"What was he selling anyway?" Angela replied.

Barbara opened the case and swore. "Bugger. Cleaning products again. Oh well, I guess we can put it up on the auction site."

"How come Janet down the road always gets the ones with the good stuff?" Angela complained, shifting back into her feline form so she could properly express her displeasure.

Myra

Not quite the worst job, but.

Myra was beyond pissed by this point. She hated working underwater, she hated being given lower torsos without legs, and she really hated working in an open helmet.

"Join the Cyborg Engineering Corps, it's great for your career!", they said.

Bollocks.

When she got back into a body that could walk, she was resigning. She had enough cash to pay out her mods, and to live on for a couple of years.

Maybe she could spend some of it hunting down the designer of this unit, and introducing them to it. Personally.

And now her non-existent foot was itching.

Bollocks.

—

Myra was pissed again. No legs. Again.

Her latest assignment had her hooked into a snake-like body. Well, snake-like from the hips down.

Yes, it gave her the ability to navigate the voids between the rockfalls, but really it was just a pain. The armoured vest helped, but not that much, and her arms kept getting in the way. Yet again, some idiot designer had come up with "a brilliant solution", and she was stuck using it.

The designer did not have to worry about what to do with his arms, or the way grit and dirt went down the front of the vest as she slithered along.

"Bollocks"

"What was that unit one?"

"Nothing control, just another awkward rock."

And she still couldn't break her contract. Maybe after this rescue.

And her list of idiot designers was getting longer.

—

Myra had done it! She'd finally managed to buy out what was left of her contract with the Cyborg Engineering Corps.

She even had legs now. Even more amazingly, they were ones that looked human, and even felt like they were real to the touch.

She looked at the spec sheet again in wonder, and her eyes wandered down to the lower left corner. What was that?

Then she recognised the mark. It was HIS. The designer who had tormented her throughout her career with CEC. The one who kept giving her bodies without legs. And HE had designed these wonders as well?

"Bollocks" What was she going to do with her little list now?

Pest Control

Ever notice whatever swarm of giant things it is out there, something is controlling it?

Locusts don't have nests or queens, so these were not locusts, for all that they swarmed and devoured like them. Jackie knew all of this, because she had studied these creatures, and tracked them back to their source.

She figured out how to trick them into letting her into the nest unharmed.

And she figured out how to get twenty tonnes of ANFO into it.

She walked away, and pressed the detonator.

Clearing the Air

Sometimes the old ways.

The ship tumbled slowly in space. There were no lights to be seen. The only hint that it was not completely dead was the temperature, and that indicated that inside would be only barely habitable.

Once it had been one of the great exploration ships, leaping from star to star in search of new worlds. Then, on one deserted planet, devoid of atmosphere, they collected a simple geological sample.

A cracked containment unit, and the moment air hit the sample, it burst apart into dust - dust that multiplied in the cool dry air of the ship. Dust that settled in people's lungs, and dissolved them from the inside out.

The survivors shut off most of the ship. They had the hydroponics unit, and could survive in the quarantined area, but engineering and the bridge were out of reach, and covered in the dust.

They could make occasional forays into the lab area, but the cleandown process was laborious, and not certain to work. So every time they came back, there was a quarantine period. The remaining crew was slowly shrinking.

Edith tried not to come into this room too often. The particulate contamination was high enough to be visible, and the protective suits were only so good.

"Somewhere in all this, she would have left a clue. Come on, Miche, talk to me." she muttered. Michelle had been gone for three years now, lost in the first few days of the dispersal. But her notes must have a clue.

Wait! There! In Miche's crabbed hand "Temp+Solv=Diss" "H_2O? Universal?"

Maybe steam could save them?

Burning Bot

Naturally there are some people taking bets.

The decision to move the Anarchist Art Festival to DC was a bold one.

What followed was even bolder. Even if it did not start that way.

Karen started it. She suggested the 80's theme. Then Ernst suggested a Completely Non Trademarked Shape Changing Bot as the Effigy To Burn. Mark was the one who suggested rockets in the arms so the fists would shoot off. Jen then suggested adding hydraulics and a control system so it could walk. While burning. With rockets.

Things kind of got a little out of control at that point.

To be fair to the organisers, having an iconic building Right There was just the final red cloth to the bull.

Mx in a Bottle

As always, read the fine print, my friend.

"Introducing the Pforrde Model ATV. Powered by compressed phlogiston, and equipped with the latest stored lightning lighting systems, this is a vehicle that will go anywhere!"

That's what the ad copy said. So we ordered one, and tested it out.

Which is how we ended up here, on the plains of Mars. Our compressor suits continue to work, but there is no sign of the colony. The only sign of life has been a small six-wheeled automate.

We are all wondering what a "NASA" is.

Two Worlds, One Centre of Emotional Attachment

Neither are composed of antimatter, so I guess they have something in common. And maybe Rae can find a nice actor who plays an engineer.

George and Xilith had been everything. Colleagues, friends, collaborators, and eventually not so much fell as amiably wandered into love.

Both were highly qualified biochemists, so they were not going to let a little matter of incompatible biologies stop them.

They were going to make a daughter, combining the best of both their vastly disparate metabolisms and structures.

It was just going to take a bit more effort than usual.

—

RaeXitchilla knew she'd not had a normal childhood. For starters most kids are not the result of ten years of genetic and biochemical tinkering by their parents, blending two incompatible lifeforms into a cohesive whole.

She had to admit they'd done a good job. Being able to shift in appearance to conform to either bauplan, and look good at it, was a plus. On the down side, all forms of teenage rebellion had to be carefully examined for possible interactions with her distinctly unique biochemistry. At least she got to see her brother struggle through it as well.

Dating had been the worst bit. When she let go, various bits of both her base forms tended to emerge. There had been the people who were revolted. There had been the fetish creeps.

And the fact that that had applied to both species was the bit that was really disappointing.

Still, there had to be someone out there. She just had to find them. Maybe there was a third intelligent life form out there. Or maybe there was someone on the two worlds.

Somewhere.

Form and Function

I guess they're just not feeling themselves.

This form was new. They knew their clutchmate had come this way. They must have a similar form now.

She. This form was 'she'. And she was looking for her brother.

More came. Places. Identifiers - names.

As the information flooded in, the structures that were began to disappear.

Rachel shook her head. Where was her little brother now?

Scale

Letter to the Editor, Proceedings of the Paramecium Philosophical Society

I hypothesize the existence of vast creatures that we and others like us live upon.

These creatures move about in knowable and unguessable ways, and interact for reasons unknown.

Have we not heard tales of great crushing darknesses falling upon us, leaving strangers in their wake? These are meetings between the great things we live upon.

Spy Troubles

That guy who can't get enough of his own awesomeness.

"Which is why I knew that the communist infiltrators held you where you were! Are you impressed by my mighty... Oh, she's passed out. Probably I was too awesome for her to bear."

"Maybe if I keep pretending to be unconscious, he'll shut up. I can't kill him until after he gets me inside his base...I can't kill him yet...I can't kill him yet..."

Public Notice

Always pay attention to the signage.

"Management would like to remind all hotel guests that all staff are to be treated with respect. Please refrain from overly familiar actions, and remember to use appropriately dignified honorifics. Despite their resemblance, it is not appropriate to refer to the senior customer relations officer as 'Mr Fluffikins', nor it is appropriate to scritch his ears."

Status Report

There may have been some mis-cataloging.

From: Southern Andes Rehab Station Five

To: Rehab Central Reporting

Subject: Quarterly Update

CO2 sequestering is ahead of schedule by 7.2%

O2 production is up 3%

H2O heavy metals are down 6% over schedule

We have had successful breeding of local bird species.

Winged reptile releases successful. They are now migrating to mountain regions. As expected, they are aiding in heavy metal sequestering.

Efforts to restore sapience to local quadrupeds so far unsuccessful. Please confirm records of wisdom.

Nature's Fury, and Glitter

Mad science demands, if not class, then style.

The night was stormy, that is true. It was also dark, being a new moon, this is also true. However, on this particular night, the, shall we say 'non-conventional' scientist was not in their laboratory, nor digging up a grave, or even playing a completely outsized keyboard.

No, xe was sitting in the window of their apartment, in town, not in some dusty castle, and were enjoying a particularly good mug of hot chocolate. After all, a good storm should be appreciated, not ignored. Even for the best of mad science.

—

The scientist looked at their lab. Alembics bubbled, great coils had sparks linking them, a large slab with restraints occupied one corner. Screens on one wall showed scenes from the great events in the world.

They pondered. Something was missing. An assistant? No, they were a solitary sort.

They looked up at the high vaulted ceiling.

A raven or a bat? No, they were no good with animals.

But, maybe. They got onto their laptop. "Mirror balls" they typed.

Two days later they looked around. Perfect!

Wardrobe Malfunction

New technology always brings challenges.

Sandra had to admit that the new nano-tech negligee did look very, very sexy. But the way it grew into her skin at various points was a little disconcerting. Not that it left her exposed in any way. The problem was taking it off. Especially in a hurry.

Abducted

Given the alternative...

Julia watched as the black-and-white police car chased after the beam carrying her up to the flying saucer. She was still low enough she was sure she'd survive the fall, and a couple of quick experiments showed that the beam could easily be escaped.

"Back to my patriarchy controlled life,or being abducted by aliens. You know? It would have been nice to be able to pack first," she said to herself as she relaxed into the beam's grasp.

Smuggled

To his credit, he did not scream.

The giant snake glared at the elegant young woman

"You know how long you've had me in that box??"

"Please, darling, I know you were asleep for almost all of that. You had that hamster to digest."

"I was still in there..."

"Dearest, you know we had to for the flight. You remember what happened last time you traveled outside."

"Stupid Jackson"

"Now dear, let me dismiss the help. Wilhelm? Here's a diamond, don't let the management know I tipped you, Ok?"

Housecall

She does not usually wear the mask, but this client is reassured by it.

Alice opened the door, and was greeted by a figure in a huge and ghastly wooden mask, carrying a dozen obsidian tipped spears.

She called out to the ogre in the oversized living room. "Darling? Your acupuncturist is here!"

The Hidden Weakness

Good help is so hard to find.
The Forest Queen looked on at the invaders to her territory with disdain. She looked to her left at her sacred guardian, and her head dropped.

Beside her, her ancient companion, protector, and enforcer of her will Mr High and Mighty Guard Wolf clearly sensed something about the invaders. And she knew all too well what happened when he detected the possibility of someone having T R E A T S. He flopped out his tongue, and rolled on his back. What is this 'dignity' of which you speak?

Gotta Go

Some people.

As the second assistant engineer, Lawrence was checking the damage to the starship after the rushed take-off.

He spotted a puddle near one of the fuel pipes.

"Hey, what's this? Have we got another lea.." he trailed off. He sniffed. Looking up, he could see the third assistant engineer dart around a corner.

"BARRY! You jerk! Couldn't you use the actual facilities, those ones that are just 20 metres away?"

Forethought and No Thought

There are heroes, and there are patsies.

"Get behind me Edith!"

"Ok..." Edith pushed on the rock, which rotated slightly. " Hold them off, Bruce, I'll get help!"

Edith did not wait for an answer, but slipped inside and closed the hidden door. "Yep, hold them off in a completely exposed position, you dolt. I really need a better class of sidekick. Maybe a robot."

Excursion Day

One of the great train trips is the Indian Pacific in Australia. It stops for a couple of hours in a ghost town in the desert. You can spot the people from highly urbanised areas, because after the first fifteen minutes or so, they start to get this look in their eyes, as they are surrounded by the emptiness of the outback, and they cluster ever closer to the entries back into the train.

The Nereid was not exactly a generation ship, but it still took twenty years to reach their destination. Only the adults knew what it was like to be on a planet.

Alex had packed their day bag. Today would be their first acclimatisation visit. Two hours down, three back, and two on the surface of the new world.

It was exciting and scary. They had been briefed on what to expect, but there were going to be some of them that could not adapt, even with therapy.

Hopefully no-one they knew. Or them.

Things You Cannot Unsee

Unseeing is not to be confused with the Unseelie.

It is said by the wise ones that all communications technologies get used for two things before all others.

The first is religion. The other is pornography.

Doctor Malkon was not immune to this truism. Upon discovering the principle of the time viewer, the first thing he did with it was to seek out the great beauties of the past.

He did not expect to find one of them making love to an early domestic Artificial Person. He certainly did not expect it to be his great grandmother!

On Break

Life models have it hard, even for photographic sessions.

The huge black dragon looked over at the white horse, who had her head down in a feed trough.

"And do you know how hard it is to hold a pose like that? I mean we are professionals and all, but these painters just don't pay us enough."

The horse looked up.

"And you do this sort of thing once, and then everyone wants to do it! Even those so called musicians with the shouty records want us to pose for *their* painters. I tell you, we should unionise," the dragon continued.

The horse resumed eating.

Launch Day

Remember, when creating a bio-mimicking vehicle, consider the gender being portrayed.

Finally it was complete! The Skywhale Masquerade Project was flying at last!

Jackie took the helm, and gave the orders "Cast off! Power to tail, one third!" The majestic vessel slowly moved off, leaving the tenders behind.

"Radar! Report!"

George replied "We are clear. Scouts report a herd 1500km SSE"

"Altering course 135 degrees port."

Now they would be able to get inside one of the herds, and really see what was going on, without the guardian whales attacking.

She hoped.

Fertility Rites

Different strokes...

The horde of skeletons looked out at the flock of vultures that descended on the battlefield.

As one they raised their undead voices:

Praise be to you, oh Maker of Bones!

We thank you for the stripping of unsightly flesh, and the bringing of New People!

Grace us now with your departure that we may welcome our new fellows to our lands!

The Forest is Just Trees

The Dark Forest hypothesis is pretty grim. Or are they looking at it wrong?

It was a great surprise to everyone when an unassuming Australian physicist worked out the equations that permitted faster-than-light travel.

It was an even greater surprise to find that the engineering required to build a device to implement the theory was found to be almost trivial. It was not even particularly expensive - a typical EV car cost more than an FTL drive unit.

In accordance with things coming in threes, there was one final surprise: Organic life could not survive the process.

It only cost the lives of five astronauts - and several dozen test animals.

Once this was proven, enthusiasm for the FTL projects around the globe dropped dramatically. But some did continue. One of the more interesting aspects of the mathematics was that the process did not involve any sort of acceleration. The device simply created a field that linked two points in space. Increasing the energy just increased the size of the object transferred.

All you had to do was define the relative coordinates of the origin and the destination.

The first probe sent further than across a room vanished. So did the next three. On a hunch, the engineering team of the fifth probe fitted a powerful transmitter, and sent it on its way. Again, the return program appeared to fail.

And then, a few minutes later, the NASA Deep Space Network reported receiving a beacon message from the probe - just inside the orbit of the moon. The probe had been gone 30 minutes.

Astronomers quickly worked out what was wrong - it was not a problem with the probe, it was because the Earth, and the Solar System had moved.

Having worked out that problem, the next probe was retrieved successfully. And then sent on the first real mission: to a point outside the Milky Way to image our home galaxy.

The probe dutifully returned several hours later, to a point far enough away to not fall to Earth, but close enough to transmit the data it had gathered. The image of the galaxy was all that the designers had hoped for.

The radio transmissions were less expected. Hundreds of them, very high powered, but all structurally the same. And only able to be picked up outside of the radio noise and gas clouds found within a galaxy.

When decoded they all basically said the same thing, in many different ways.

"Is there anyone here?"

The Ex

Marian used to rock the Golightly look.

Sacha looked out the window, and pulled the curtain shut at once.

"Oh no, Mike! It is my ex! And he's got Marian's head"

Mike snatched a quick glance, and saw an approaching postman topple and shatter.

"Sacha, I know you said Marian had killer looks, but I didn't think you meant literally!"

Parking

Ah...family.

The spaceship bounced off a stationary freighter, and rammed the docking port gantry.

Penny glared at Sarah. "You know Steve can't parallel park."

"I do now, Penny. He said he'd been practicing."

"Why do you keep believing him, Sarah?"

"Well, he is my twin brother."

"Mirror twin. From an alternative universe."

"Is that why you don't trust Peter?"

Penny sighed. "I do trust him, but he's me with the guard rails off."

"You girls know we are right here, don't you?" Peter interrupted.

Dowsing

When does the label become the thing?

He looked down again, blindfold pushed up on his head. Pointing dead ahead. He'd successfully dowsed what he believed subconsciously was real water.

Huh. So this is what it has come to.

Grandma always said it relied on the power of belief. And it looked like advertising and the net had become the default belief system of the world, at least if this was anything to go by.

The rod was pointing at an ad for a restaurant.

"I guess they have water in there."

The Worst Job

This runs a close second for a horror story.

Cynthia was bored. Who wouldn't be?

"Level 12956 - Pre-Teen Fashions"

When they built the SkyHook, they never thought about what would happen next.

"Level 12957 - Early Teen Fashions"

Some bright spark had the idea of a new department store, didn't they?

"Level 12958 - Mid Teen Fashions and Mental Health Consulting"

Which led to this job. Lift operator. For the tallest department store in the world.

"Level 12959 - Mid Teen Parental Mental Health Consulting"

God, she was bored.

There's Always One

It does not matter what you are, there is always a Larry.

The red eyed robot spoke ominously "Humans! We have agreed that..."

The green eyed one broke in "Oh boy! Organic life forms! Do you know how long it has been since I've seen an organic life form? It must be ... Oh, minutes! That's like forever for us, what with how fast our brains run. Hey are you going"

"Larry."

"To do some of your sports? Howabout one of your mating rituals? Or maybe eat"

"LARRY!"

"Huh? What? I'm just so excited!"

"Larry, we are supposed to be delivering the ultimatum."

"What ultimatum? Do we have one? What is it?"

The red-eyed robot shook its head.

The female human spoke "Err, do you want to come back later?"

Pop

The horror, the horror...

For days the huge alien had observed the Earth, refusing to respond to any form of communication. The immense spherical being just hung in the sky, watching.

Finally someone had had enough, and fired on it. Not the army, not some science group, no, just some guy with the wrong amount of knowledge and skills.

And so, the giant sentient beach ball looked on in horror as the terrifyingly pointy model rocket screamed towards its skin!

If You Have to Ask...

Ah, the incomparable Kate Bush.

Mounted on her battle cricket, Helga charged towards the dragonworm.

At the last moment, she drew upon her deepest powers, and assaulted the creature with a barrage of interpretive dance!

Later she credited her victory to the training of her teacher, Mistress Bush.

Waking the Vigilante Boss

This probably explains a lot about Alfred, too.

Dhaby knew it was time for Shelby to get up. He also knew what happened to him the last time. His back still gave him trouble.

This time he was going to use a stick. Shelby couldn't headlock him that way.

Later that day...

"Dhaby, why are you walking funny?" asked his assistant.

"Shelby. And I don't want to talk about it."

Awards Night

The aerospace fighter blasted shells at the kaiju, and missed.

"No, George, the *nails*, you are supposed to be hitting the nails!"

"Ok, Justine, if you're so hot, you take the shot!"

Justine slid into the firing seat, took aim, and flawlessly painted all eight nails.

Then she took the mic.

"There! You will be going to the ball tonight!"

Survey

A love letter to automated probes everywhere.

The control unit was annoyed, as it usually was on these missions.

"WX6 finish getting yourself deployed from CRU2! We've got work to do!

WX7, you get going on the camera work, CRU1, establish uplink to ORU. WX6, you start running the chemistries.

We've got an air temperature half way between freezing and boiling water, so we are unlikely to find life, but we have to try."

—

"Yeah, we saw some odd lights last night Agent Brown, but this is Death Valley, ya get weird stuff all the time. Seeya."

—

Report: Barely habitable. No complex life.

A New Hero

The idea of a superhero who does not give a toss tickles me.

The siege of the bank had been going on for hours. Scores of police blocked off the street, and on top of a nearby building a TV news crew broadcast the standoff to a waiting nation.

Then the crew noticed movement. A young woman, dressed in a black skirt,leather vest, and Doc Martins, wearing headphones, was making her way through the police lines. She spoke to no-one, but no-one tried to stop her. She walked up to the front door of the bank, and went inside.

After a few minutes, the bank robbers and the hostages all started filing out, most of them with their heads hung low, some crying. One of the bank robbers raised a gun to his own head, and then just gave up, dropped it, and sat down, head in his hands.

From the flanks, the police moved in and secured everyone. The police in the centre did nothing at all. A few of them had likewise sat down and appeared to be oblivious to what was going on around them.

The news crews closed in.

Getting a coherent story out of anyone proved difficult. Most people just asked what the point was. Some shrugged and said nothing at all. Eventually the news crews pieced together what had happened. Wherever the young woman had walked, people around her were struck with a sense of hopelessness, despair, or just all consuming apathy. Those on the edges were least affected, those closest, the most.

The rooftop news crew kept watch as the crowds slowly dispersed. After an hour or so the mystery woman walked out, looked around, looked up at the news crew and gave them the finger. Then she walked off, the world just a little greyer and duller as she passed.

The city had a new hero. The Goth. And she didn't care.

Cooked Out

Look up LOX BBQ. You won't be disappointed. Also, do not get confused making bagels and lox.

The starship had landed, and the crew were making the most of being able to walk around outside of the ship. As evening rolled around they had established a secure energy fence line around the landing site, and decided to relax and celebrate their temporary freedom.

The party was just getting started, and everyone was just starting to relax when there was a massive ball of fire from where the BBQ had used to be.

Phil immediately knew what had happened and yelled "Mike, we warned you about putting LOX on the BBQ. Now what are we going to do for dinner?"

Timing is Everything

Oops.

"Honey, I know you're from my future, but you have to understand - I'm from yours!"

"What?"'

"I'd hoped to catch you before I left."

"But that was what I was planning!"

"Well poo."

Bronze Chefs

We all know how this looks.

Panonis roared, the silver studs on the black leather of his harness glinting in the desert light, the leather dark as night against his deep red skin. He drew his arm back.

Khadon snarled as Panonis smashed the pomegranate against his chest, splattering seeds across his armour. He drew his khopesh.

"Curse your barbaric ways! You should cut the top and bottom off, and then divide into segments!"

Their battles over cooking techniques became legend.

Feeding the Bridge

It never hurts to know the "Why?".

It is a popular thing to watch the local news reports for word of a truck losing a fight with some bridge or another, and having to be towed away.

Some more observant people will notice that such low-hanging structures are, to turn a phrase, uncommonly common. And that no matter what protections are put in place, vehicles will still get stuck.

What only a very few people notice is that almost every city will have at least one such structure. And if it is modified or removed, some other structure will be built to take its place.

The reason for this ties into the reason trucks will always get stuck there.

You see it is not trolls that live under bridges, but sirens. A siren's call cannot be denied, hence the accidents. And the new construction, for if a siren loses her home, she will enchant some architect into building a new one.

What do the sirens get out of the crashes? The sound. They are creatures of sound, and the sound of crashing metal feeds them.

Late Cretaceous Open Mic Night

I'm sure you can dig this guy up somewhere.

A claw reaches out and taps the mic. "Hey is this thing on? OK, so howabout this whole asteroid thing, I reckon it is being blown up all out of proportion. I mean, a giant rock? I eat giant rocks for breakfast. Well, with breakfast, anyway. Helps with the digestion. So I think if there is a giant one coming this way, what we need to do is set up a nice big buffet, so we've got some use for it!"

There is some applause, and a bit of roaring.

"Thank-you. Oh yeah, and what is with these mammals popping up? "

A Slight Miscalculation

Sometimes no comment is the best comment.

OK, so the transformation potion worked fine. I even got to keep my thumbs, just as I planned.

What I had not planned on was the different geometry of a cat's forelegs. Or the lack of fingerprints. Claws are great, but they suck at gripping hard surfaces.

Opening the bottle of antidote is going to take some work.

Santa's Lot

It is a popular mathematical experiment to try and work out just how fast Santa has to be to reach every house with a child in a single 24 hour period.

The calculations always end up with a significant fraction of the speed of light.

There then usually follow discussions about what the collateral damage from Santa's passing would be. And cargo limits, and so on.

All of these are wrong, and ignore another end-of-year tradition. The portrayal of the ending year as an old man.

Now that I've put these two traditions side-by-side, I think you can see what is really going on.

It is possible for one man to visit every house in a night, with no shock waves or any of that silliness. But it comes at a cost.

For that man, the night lasts many years, as he travels back in time after each visit. Even with time travel, he does not get much time to eat - so the snacks you leave out are essential to him surviving the night.

But he only just survives. By the end of the night he will have aged over forty years. And then he hands the reins of the time-traveling sleigh to a younger man, warning him of the cost.

Someone always answers the call, despite the cost, because there is always someone willing to sacrifice everything to bring joy and light, even just a little, even if only for a moment.

So leave the snacks, and, if you catch a glimpse of him, give him a bow of respect. He deserves it.

Scout and Shaman

This is one of my longer works, and the only story here that originates before I started posting on Mastodon. There are two things here of note: One, yes I have filed the serial numbers off a vintage SF RPG for the concepts used in the setting. Two, you deserve a special round of applause if you can figure out what music video was the inspiration.

Lorn was having a really bad day.

It had started out normally enough - jump in, run radio and spectrographic scans on the highest-probability planet, the usual procedures for a scout checking out a new system. The scans had come back with a good 02/N2 mix, decent hydrographics, and only the usual background noise in RF.

There were tags showing chlorophyll based plants - generally a good sign that the ecology was going to be broadly human-compatible.

She was checking those results when the targeting alarm went off. Somewhere another ship had lit her up with radar, and the only reason for that would be - there - heat plumes, accelerating fast.

Missiles.

And more of them than her little scout ship could hope to deal with. She was too close to the planet to jump, and not fast enough to outrun them. She had one chance.

Using pure brute force, her little ship killed as much of the orbital velocity as it could, and Lorn set the autopilot on a fast re-entry. Looking at the figures, it was still not going to save the ship from the missiles, but it might be enough to save her.

As her ship hit the atmosphere, a ball of plasma formed, and Lorn left the tiny bridge. In the aft hold, an even tinier floater sat. Normally used for exploring planetary surfaces, it was not intended for high-altitude work. Tugging on her helmet, she quickly strapped in, and hit the emergency hatch release at the same time as releasing the hold-downs.

The blast of air tossed the floater out, and into the maelstrom of plasma, the gravitics providing a wafer-thin shield as Lorn drove them to maximum power - and then she was clear. Moments later, an even dozen missiles flashed past her, and slammed into her ship, only a handful of kilometres away. The resulting blast shattered the scoutship into countless fragments.

—

Finder-of-Unnoticed-Details was having a good day.

Her tribe had moved on to the next stage of the annual migration, and she would join them in a day or two. For now, she was content to wait.

Last night she had seen a new star appear. This was not unusual, but unlike the others, it had not been followed by a long needle-cloud, and the arrival of the sky raiders. This one had stopped and drifted across the sky. It rose several times throughout the night, always content to drift from horizon to horizon. As it did, she looked to the lake, watched the insects, and her mind drifted.

In the distance, her tribe. Further away, her family's tribe. Further still, trading partners, rivals, and there! A single faint glimmer. Searching, questioning, seeking answers. A scholar? No, an explorer.

A scholar as well, but at her heart an explorer.

Finder was intrigued, to say the least.

Finally, as dawn approached, and the star bearing the explorer made another pass, it suddenly changed direction, swooped across the sky, and erupted into a mass of fire and fragments. And a continuing gem of bright fierce focus.

The mass of fire and debris continued across the sky, vanishing in the direction of the copper diggers. The bright gem of focussed thought, though, that was following a different path, and not entirely one of the explorer's choosing.

The valley beyond the forest. That is where it will come to rest, Finder decided. Standing, she gestured to her horse, and, when he came to her, whispered in his ear, and he trotted off towards the forest.

Explorer or not, someone was going to be feeling very alone soon. And Finder-of-Unnoticed-Details knew exactly how to fix that.

She gathered her clothes, dressed, and started slowly walking after her horse.

—

Finder-of-Unnoticed-Details was having a bad day.

Lorn had closed herself off from her. Hiding her mind was one of the first things Finder had taught her, knowing that the sky-raiders could follow such things as well as she could. But usually she did not, knowing that Finder took comfort in feeling the spark of her mind.

But now she was hiding that spark, even though there were no raiders. And she'd been doing it for days.

She'd seen Lorn going through the things she had salvaged from her wrecked craft. The tiny fragile thing that had saved her from the raider's weapons. Very little of it worked, but Lorn kept it all the same. Maybe she'd worked out how to fix the wreck and was leaving. That thought broke Finder's heart.

She watched as Lorn, now dressed in a hunter's leathers, worked through the salvage, apparently unaware of Finder's distress.

—

Lorn was having a good day.

Mostly.

She did not like causing Finder pain in this way, but shutting herself off was the only way she could do what she was planning without Finder knowing ahead of time.

Not much of the little grav floater had survived being used as an impromptu lifeboat when her ship had been blown up, but the power supply still worked, even after five years, and so did one of the grav modules. Not enough to lift anything, but she could focus the field and invert it.

Using this she took the coal she'd obtained from the tribe of miners to the east, and used the module to compress the two lumps. While that took place, she took some of the fibre cabling and wove it with some copper wire from the southern tribes, combined with some hairs from the tail of Finder's stallion.

The whole process took nearly a seven day, by which time Finder was almost beside herself, but, wonder that she was, she said nothing and asked nothing, even though Lorn could tell it was eating her alive.

It was finally done, though, and Lorn went to where Finder was staring out over the lake.

"Finder."

"Lorn."

"I know I have been closed to you for this past sevenday..."

"I have seen you working on your flying machine. You are leaving."

"I have been working on something, but not that." Lorn brought out the two necklaces she had constructed. Optical fibres from the sky, copper wire from the earth, horsehair from the tribe, and tiny bright stones, like stars. "May I be yours, and you mine?" she asked, finally letting her mind open again.

Finder was almost knocked over by the intensity of Lorn's mind, focused entirely on her being, on her heart.

She did not say anything, just stared, and then, slowly reached over and took one of the necklaces and placed it around Lorn's neck. Then she lowered her head.

Lorn took the hint, and lowered the other necklace over Finder's head. Finder looked up, eyes that were usually so knowing and calm full of tears, wonder, and joy.

"Yes."

—

Both Finder-of-Unnoticed-Details and Lorn-from-the-Sky were having a day. One that was both good and bad.

In the seven years since Lorn had arrived on this world - whose name roughly translated to 'Mother-of-all' in the local language, she had heard many tales of the 'sky raiders'. Indeed, her own arrival was due to those same raiders, but in the last seven years they had not raided within the sphere of Finder's tribe.

That had changed this morning.

Unlike previous raids, though, this time they had warning, thanks to the equipment salvaged from the wreck of Lorn's grav floater. It had not been much. A partially working radio system, a single gravitic module, a survival kit, which did include a small laser pistol. And a micro reactor - fed water, it produced more power than the handful of equipment could use.

Of all of these, the radio was the important one this morning. The pistol was intended for hunting light game - it would be useless against someone with even the most trivial of armour. But six hours warning? A wealth beyond imagining. Especially with the tribe being able to push a warning out to the other tribes in the region.

And so the raiders came down, and found no-one and nothing. Not even their mind seekers could find anything. And they were searching.

Lorn and Finder were confident that the tribes would not be found. They had long ago, long before Lorn's arrival, devised hiding places the raiders could not find or reach. This was not where Finder and Lorn were though. Prior to arriving, Lorn had been a Scout. And, in her heart, she still was, for all that she wore a hunter's leathers instead of her shipsuit. And Scouts learned about things. Especially threats.

So here they were, watching over the raiders' landing area by the lake. A hose ran from the lake to the ship, sucking in water to fuel the reactors. And what a ship. Lorn would have guessed it to be eight times the size of her tiny and sadly missed Scoutship. If it had been much larger it would have had trouble landing. It was heavily armed, too, with a mix of lasers and missile racks.

There were thirty of them. Mostly human, with a couple of alien forms among them. Well armed with laser long arms, but only stab vests for armour.

As they watched, there was some sort of commotion, and one of them started yelling and waving, and all of them started running towards the ship.

Finder looked at Lorn with a questioning expression. She just shrugged in reply. Within minutes the raiders had returned to the ship, and a few minutes later it lifted off, leaving the hoses behind.

Once the ship had vanished over the horizon, Lorn turned to Finder.

"I could not hear what they were saying, but it sounded like Anglic."

"Your people?"

"Well, people from the same place. They were not Scouts or Navy. I wonder." Finder could feel her thoughts spike "Let's get to the tunnels, I need to check the radio!"

—

The pirate cruiser was having a bad day.

Normally this dirtball was a good place to refuel and grab some fresh food. The local population were bronze-age at best, and the ecology was human compatible without any processing. And no-one came here.

There had been that scout seven years ago, but they had been quickly disposed of.

But now, there was a whole fleet of ships here. And one of them was ten times the size of their little cruiser.

On the positive side for the pirates, it was not going to be a very long day.

—

Gordon Haultmann was having a good day. The depot ship he led and the ships it supported had arrived in this virgin system just a few hours ago, and was surprised to detect radio transmissions from the primary candidate world.

He was even more surprised when they detected a ship departing the planet.

Surprise did not even begin to describe things when they received a very basic transmission from the planet with two components - the word "Pirates" and a scout ID. One that was listed as "MIA".

Dispatching the pirate ship was barely a flicker from the massive batteries of the depot ship.

The transmission from the surface then became a homing beacon.

—

Lorn and Finder watched the new stars - "Starships" Lorn called them, as if they were kin to the barges that travelled the river.

Her kin.

One of them broke ranks, and vanished over the horizon. Half an hour later there was a distant sound of thunder. "Sonic boom".

Not long after the arrow-head shaped craft came into view. An eighth of the size of the raider's craft - the smallest possible. Identical to the one that brought Lorn to the Mother-of-All. And to Finder.

"Come on, let's see who has come to visit!" Lorn excitedly said.

"You do not know?" was Finder's much more subdued reply.

"Nope. I don't recognise that artwork. She's active duty, though. Those markings on the nose are the deployment group."

"Lorn, these are your people, not mine. Will they..."

"My heart, they will have thought me dead these last three years at least. And if I choose to settle here, they cannot change that."

"But?"

"They will want to talk to me. And to you. And the elders, and the copper diggers, and everyone else."

"And then?"

"They'll leave. They might leave me a fresh beacon and other gear, but they won't stay. This is our home, not theirs."

"We have old stories about ships like that."

"So do we. We eventually learn."

Tugging on Finder's hand, Lorn started towards the ship.

Finder let her mind go ahead of her, and was surprised to feel a mix of excitement, curiosity, and hope. It seemed that these new arrivals did know Lorn after all.

Finder smiled behind Lorn's back. Let this be a surprise for her.

Shaman Scout

A sequel to the preceding story. I would just like to say that I would hope when we do reach the stars, we are as enlightened.

Joyful Finder sat on the grassy hillside and watched the horses, feeling their emotions. They felt safe and well fed. One of the mares was feeling slowed and heavy with her coming foal.

As she watched she thought about her family's history. Although her clan went back thousands of years, her family really started a mere two hundred years ago, when her great-great-great grandparents had met.

Since then the star people had kept their word. Oh, there were occasional visits, but only to replenish the small cache of emergency supplies they had negotiated permission to stash for shipwrecked spacefarers. And once, long ago, to bring news to her ancestor of her parents' passing.

During that time her people had developed from isolated clans to a series of interconnected towns, with railways linking them. Innovations that the clans had had the capability to do for many centuries, but had chosen not to develop until recently.

There was even talk of building flying machines.

Why all these changes? While the star people had kept their word, the clans had not been idle in extracting news and gossip of the wider universe from them. Not that most of them were aware of it. The few who were, well a couple of them stayed. The rest understood. And things were changing out in the stars. The clans needed to be ready in case raiders returned.

Which is why Joy was sitting here on a hillside. Earlier that day the ancient sensor array that her ancestor had set up had noted the arrival of a ship from her ancestor's people. Time to make a choice.

Joy stood, and sent a suggestion to the horses to move into the woods. The arriving ship would not panic them there. Then she walked down to the field, and started spreading chalk into a series of shapes taken from Lorn's books.

Setting out the pattern took most of the morning. Taking a break for a light snack and a drink, she surveyed her handiwork with the help of her favourite hunting bird. It was good, and well timed, too. A brief conference, and the bird landed on her shoulder. Dives Swiftly insisted that Joy needed her to look after her.

The arrowhead shaped spaceship landed in the centre of the marked grid, and the usual single figure emerged. This one was not human, although they were still bipedal.

Joy shrugged, stood, and approached. Now she had to convince them to take her with them, and to learn the ways of the star peoples' scouts.

—

Joyful Finder was not feeling a lot of joy at what she had found. Neither was Dives Swiftly, her hunting bird companion.

The Scout training base had been OK. She'd even made some friends amongst the many peoples that made up the service. But now she'd been given her first assignment. And it was not one that impressed her.

Postal service.

Yes, it was an essential service, and one that the highly independent Scouts were well prepared to provide, but bouncing back and forth between two systems for the next few years was not going to help her get anywhere near home.

And for Dives Swiftly it was going to be horrible. Even knowing that, the fierce bird was not going to leave Joy to her own devices. Who knew what sort of trouble she could get into without Dives' beak and claws? Dives knew that she had been a major factor in Joy's academic success. Even the other students had noticed the stern mothering the bird directed at her human.

But, for now, they were being shipped like cargo to their home for the next few years. Every three months they'd get a few days break, but it was going to be a long time before they got to move to another assignment.

—

Their little postal courier was surprisingly roomy - not enough space for Dives to hunt in, but at least she'd be able to fly some. And it was relatively new - only a few years old. But there was only her cabin and the bridge really. Oh, there were access ways and such in the engineering area, but not somewhere someone could live for a week or more. They were going to be on their own.

Joy shook herself, and got settled. The data banks would be filling already with transmissions from the world below - and from other ships in the area. Very few of these would be for the world she was going to, most would be sent to the courier waiting for her arrival, and then to another, and another, until the messages reached their destinations.

Meantime, when she was not piloting, Joy would be studying, learning more to take back to her people. And saving funds to purchase equipment.

The radio came to life "Courier Gamma Whiskey Echo Three Seven Niner, confirm receipt."

She checked the logs, and replied "Tender Charlie Gamma Echo Five One One, I confirm receipt."

"Very good, you are clear for departure."

"Thank you Charlie Gamma, see you in a fortnight."

Joy checked the navigation instruments, the star drive status, and the rest of the checklist. Then she hit a button and the world turned inside out and back again.

There, they were on their way. In a week they'd appear at their destination, and a tender would come out to them with fuel and fresh supplies, and then she'd make the same journey backwards.

The exciting life of the postie.

—

It had been sixteen long years since Joyful Finder had been home. Given the changes she'd seen even while growing up, she imagined it would have changed even more in the time she'd been away.

Dives Swiftly watched her hands move over the controls as her little ship emerged back into normal space about a day out from her home, and then pecked the radio scanner speaker control.

There was a burst of static, and then words - in her own language! A weather report for the jungle regions of the north-west. They must have succeeded in building satellite launchers. That at least would give raiders a little bit of pause.

Her little ship would not count for much in a fight, but what Joy carried was far more important. Twelve of those sixteen years away had been spent doing postal runs. Living almost constantly in a ship that had, really, only two components - a FTL engine, and massive computer stores. Such a life featured many long periods of doing nothing. And so she'd filled it with study - learning everything she could about kickstarting industry.

Her people had made great strides in the years since her ancestors had made a family, but there were two things that would allow them to fight effectively. The first was fusion power. Small, portable, and powerful fusion power. The second was gravitic control. With those two it was possible to build defence ships that could fight on equal terms with most raiders.

This was what she was bringing home.

Dives Swiftly pecked another control and whistled. That sounded like air traffic control. She'd call in soon.

As a teenager, Joy had looked back at her ancestor's journals. Lorn had been surprised at the depth of scientific knowledge that her adopted world had, given its largely agrarian appearance. In the two hundred years since the elders had decided to implement much of that knowledge. Now Joy would be adding to it.

Picking up the mic, she transmitted "Shaman's Home ATC, this is Scout Ship Lorndottire, Joyful Finder commanding. I am on approach to the planet, ETA to low orbit is twenty three hours."

It would be a good five to ten minutes before a reply came in.

"We'll be home soon. And you'll have a chance to hunt proper food!"

She got a whistle, and a strong sense of focus formed in her mind.

The radio crackled to life. "Shaman's Home ATC, this is Scout Ship Chorus, Charlie Fischer commanding. I am on approach to the planet, ETA to low orbit 24 hours." There was a pause. "Hello there, Lorndottire! Fancy meeting you here."

There was a sudden sense of humour coming from Dives Swiftly.

Glaring at her companion "Charlie? What are you doing here?"

"Did you think I was going to let you disappear off without me? I've been chasing you for the last fifteen systems!"

Joy smiled, and then looked back at the bird busily preening. "You knew, didn't you?" Dives looked up as if to say "Who me?", and went back to preening.

—

It was simultaneously completely ordinary, and utterly extraordinary for Joyful Finder to be following a scheduled approach plan. 'Ordinary' in that this was what she had done scores of times before during her career with the Scout service. 'Extraordinary' in that she was doing this on her homeworld, which did not even have flying machines when she'd left sixteen years previously.

As she approached the designated landing area, the cameras on the outside of her ship's hull showed a neat row of light aircraft. Mostly wood and fabric it seemed, but there was one made of metal. More remarkable was the tall gantry at the edge of the airfield, with a tall cone-topped cylinder next to it.

The learning she was bringing home would make such devices obsolete - but would be so much harder to build. All the same, if the Elders kept up the pace she was seeing, it might not take that long.

And then there was the problem of Charlie. Technically this was a quarantine world - no contact to be made. Of course the reality was somewhat different - her ancestor had settled here after being shot out of the sky by pirates. And there was an emergency supply station run by the Scouts. She was allowed to land because this was her home. Charlie would be technically breaking the treaty the Scouts had with the Elders. And interstellar law.

But they had followed Joy here. Over six months journey from where she knew they had been deployed last. She was going to have to talk to them face-to-face. And tell them the big secret she'd been hiding the whole time she'd worked with the Scouts. That it was not training that led Dives Swiftly to obey her so well. It was the fact that the two of them could communicate mind-to-mind. And that she could do that with people, too.

If Charlie could take that revelation, then there might be a way through this.

—

Charlie was not hugely surprised when the landing field informed them that they were not to leave their ship after landing. Technically they were not meant to be here. Joy could get away with it because this was her home. Charlie was an outsider, from the great interstellar conglomerate that had spawned the Scouts.

The airwaves had been silent since they had landed. There were people moving around, but no transmissions from the control centre. In fact, there were no local transmissions at all.

A sudden thought, and Charlie activated the security cameras, and scanned around the ship. No-one. But the views did offer some insight as to the goings on outside. They could see small teams moving equipment from a hanger to one of the aircraft. Elsewhere, someone was pumping fuel. All perfectly ordinary for an airfield of this level of development. Except there was the rocket launchpad at one end. One that was clearly capable of handling orbital-class chemical rockets. That was out of place.

While they were studying the launch zone, there was a sudden banging on the forward hatch. A check of the cameras showed Joy with her ever-present pet Dives waiting.

They opened the hatch, and the two visitors entered the ship and made their way to the bridge.

"Joy! It is so good to see you again" there was nothing forced in the welcome "I know -" Charlie broke off as the flying predator that was Joy's pet suddenly launched itself into the air, straight at their face! They barely got their arm up when it made the slightest of turns and shot past, one wingtip barely brushing their elbow. It landed on the control board, and started strutting about. Then it stopped, looked back at Joy, and looked about the panel. It stalked over to one end, flipped up a cover, and before Charlie could say or do anything, pulled the main circuit breaker out.

The emergency lights came on, flooding the room with a pale yellowish glow. "Thank-you Dives" said Joy.

Charlie stared at her.

"Sorry Charlie, I had to make sure the CVR and everything else was shut down, so I asked Dives Swiftly to pull the breaker. I'll help you reset everything once we've spoken." She dropped into the co-pilot's chair. "I'll explain everything."

Charlie, lost for words, waved a hand.

"Did I ever tell you about my distant ancestor who was a Scout?" She got a nod, and continued "Lorn crashed not far from here, and then a horse turned up with a saddle and bridle." Joy retold the story of Lorn and Finder. "Now does any of that sound odd to you?"

"Um... How did the horse get there?"

"Finder sent it."

"Oh. Wait, from how far away? About half a day's walk? And the horse just went up to a complete stranger?"

"Because Finder asked it to."

"But horses are not sentient. Are they?"

"No, but Finder had a trick up her sleeve. She could show the horse exactly what she wanted it to do."

"How?"

Then Charlie froze, as they not-quite-heard a faint voice softly whisper "Like this" accompanied by an image of Dives Swiftly perched on their shoulder. There was a whistle from behind, a flap, and a sudden weight next to their head. Dives ducked their head down and gave a low, soft, confidential whistle into Charlie's ear.

They carefully looked to the left. A bright yellow eye looked back. "You're telepathic?"

"Yes. A few of us are. We mainly use it to befriend animal

companions, but we can, with practice, detect feelings from a distance and send messages."

"So that's why you killed the recorders. But why tell me?"

"You landing here - even jumping into the system - is a breach of the Treaty. But there is a way around it. And given you were willing to travel for over half a year to catch up to me, I figure it is probably a goer. But if we are going to go down that path, I had to come clean."

"So you know..."

"I'm guessing. It would be very rude of me to actually look into a friend without asking."

"And how do you feel about it?"

Joy got up, took one step, leaned close to Charlie, asked "May I?", and getting a nod, kissed them deeply.

There was one way a Scout could stay on this planet. And that was to become part of one of the clans.

About the Author

Rob Masters is a long time fan of science fiction and fantasy, a keen role-player, and long time supporter of both local fan-run conventions.

Professionally he is an IT generalist, working with Free and Open Source systems. He is employed as a systems administrator.

His other interests include life-long passions for boating and photography, a fondness for strange human-powered vehicles, and board-gaming.

He maintains an active presence on Mastodon, and has an infrequently updated blog at https://rdmasters.lympago.com .

You will almost always find him in the company of his wife and partner in crime, Leece. They live in Western Australia.